HUNTING THE MIRROR MAN

BRIAN SHEA

TY HUTCHINSON

SEVERN RIVER PUBLISHING

Severn River Publishing
www.SevernRiverBooks.com

This is a work of fiction. Names, characters, businesses, places, events and incidents are either the products of the author's imagination or used in a fictitious manner. Any resemblance to actual persons, living or dead, or actual events is purely coincidental.

ISBN: 978-1-64875-383-1 (Paperback)

ALSO BY THE AUTHORS

To find out more, visit

severnriverbooks.com/series/sterling-gray-fbi-profiler

1

The little boy crept quietly down the creaky staircase to the basement, hesitating on every step as he waited for a voice to shout out "Off limits!"

But each step was met with silence.

Still dressed in his one-suit pj's, he continued, sliding his hand along the wooden banister. The air in the basement was colder than the rest of the house, and it smelled like a wet towel to him. He'd only ventured down to the basement a couple times until he was caught and given a severe beating. "Rules are in place for a reason," the man had told him after the first punch.

But at six years old, the boy's curiosity often got the best of him.

"I hear you," a man's voice called out from the basement.

The boy sucked in a breath and froze on the steps, wondering if he should turn around immediately or wait a moment or so.

"Come down, boy. It's time you learn."

Learn? He was unsure if it was a threat or an invitation.

"Snap to it. We ain't got all day."

When the boy reached the last step, he saw the man who took care of him. He peered at the boy over his black-framed glasses.

"Get over here," he said.

The man stood next to a long, narrow table made out of steel. It was high enough off the ground that the boy couldn't see the top of it. He was also shirtless and dressed in the green rubber overalls he used for fishing. He had the same ratty ball cap on his head that he always wore and the sides of his face and neck were slick with perspiration.

The boy walked over to the edge of the table. Not once did the man take his eyes off the boy. Behind the man was a wooden workstation. Hanging on the pegboard were a variety of tools. They were neatly aligned and kept in pristine condition as if they'd never been used. But they had. The boy often sat at the top of the basement stairs listening to the man grunt while using them.

"Bring that milk crate over here and step up on it so you can see," he said as he pointed across the room.

The boy walked over to the crate, pushed against the far wall, and scooted it across the concrete floor. Once next to the table, the boy climbed up on top and was surprised to find that the table wasn't flat like the table they ate dinner at. This one looked like a big sink. And lying inside of it was a naked woman . . . sleeping.

The boy drew a sharp breath, as he'd never seen an undressed woman. He glanced up at the man for direction, but none came. The boy looked back at the woman and took in all the details. She had orange hair, and freckles dotted her nose and cheeks. Her lips were pink with a light blue tint to them. Her skin was fair, free of blemishes and scars, from what he could see. He was too embarrassed to look at her breasts, thinking the man would know and yell at him for it. Her stomach was flat, and she had a piercing in her belly button. He'd seen that before on a few girls at the lake. Her privates were covered with the same-colored hair as her head. Again the boy made sure not to dawdle in that area and quickly moved his eyes down her legs, settling on her feet. She had purple nail polish on her toenails.

"Who is she?" the boy said softly.

"Does it matter?"

He shook his head, and before he realized what he was doing, he had reached out toward the woman. The tips of his fingers were an inch away from her stomach when he caught himself and stopped. He looked at the man, but he said nothing and, more importantly, gave no visual signal for the boy to stop.

He placed his hand on the woman. Her body was cool to the touch, not warm like he'd expected she'd be.

"Do you like it?" the man asked.

The boy nodded as he kept his gaze on the woman.

"Does she make you feel good inside?" the man asked. "Are you tingling?"

The boy nodded again.

"Good. It must do that to you."

The man reached into a small metal container on top of his workstation and removed a small instrument that the boy had never seen before.

"Do you know what this is?" The man held it in front of the boy, giving him a clear look at it. The fluorescent lights above glinted off the tip. "It's called a scalpel. It makes exact cuts."

The boy smiled..

"Are you ready to learn?"

The boy looked the man directly in his eyes. "I'm ready."

2

SEVENTEEN YEARS LATER

The young woman jerked awake with a sharp breath. Her eyelids fluttered briefly before gaining focus, allowing her mind to discern her whereabouts. Nothing had changed. She was still locked inside a cage.

Her breaths were hot, her mouth was dry, and her throat scratched when she swallowed. Perspiration bubbled along her arms, and her clothing felt damp against her skin. She lifted her head, peeling her cheek off the linoleum floor before pushing herself up to a sitting position. The flashbacks came quick.

She remembered the small convenience store she had walked out of.

She remembered it was late, after eleven.

She remembered how cool and pleasant the night air was.

She remembered the car stopping next to her as she walked along the side of the road.

She remembered the kind voice from inside asking for directions.

She remembered leaning into the car from the front passenger-side window.

She remembered the snapping punch to her face, her hair being pulled, and her body being yanked into the vehicle.

She remembered him grunting as he struck her repeatedly, and his heavy breathing, and the smell—woodsy cologne.

Those details and more were burned into her memory. The only thing she couldn't remember, not even the tiniest bit, was what her attacker looked like.

The cage reminded her of a dog kennel, except it was bolted to the cement floor. It was roughly five feet tall, five feet long, and four feet wide. A large padlock kept the cage door secured. Next to her was an empty water bottle, which she could not recall if she had drunk from or not. But the most unexpected thing about the cage was the classroom desk chair inside it.

The fluorescent lights on the ceiling buzzed softly as they cast their glow across the room, giving her a clear look at her surroundings. Directly opposite the cage, a whiteboard hung on the drywall. A couple dry-erase markers and erasers lined the aluminum holder. Below the whiteboard was a small lab table with storage cabinets. A pen and a pad of paper sat on top of it. Off to the left side of the room, pushed flush against a wall, was a gurney. She could only see the wheeled legs, but the rest of it was covered with a gray sheet. She thought it strange and wondered why it was there. More importantly, what was the oblong thing under the sheet? There were no windows in the room and only one closed door, presumably leading out.

She couldn't remember the drive to wherever she was. But she did remember the rough handling as she was brought into a dark room and thrown into the cage.

The sound of a door closing in the distance followed by faint whistling pulled the young woman from her thoughts. The tune was familiar: "Heigh-Ho" from *Snow White and the Seven Dwarfs*. A moment later, the door opened, and in walked a young man with his lips puckered.

He was dressed in tan khakis with a blue button-down tucked inside the waistband. His light brown hair was parted neatly on the side. He wore gold wire-framed glasses and kept his face clean-shaven. He walked over to the whiteboard, paying no attention to her, and picked up a marker. In large block letters, he wrote MR. BOWEN. BIOLOGY 101: THE HUMAN BODY.

He capped the pen, placed it back on the holder, and turned around to face the young woman.

"My name is Mr. Bowen. Welcome to my class. Student, please take your seat," he said.

Why did he call me "student"? She glanced at the desk chair and then back at Bowen, thinking he had to be joking. But the look on his face told her he was, in fact, serious.

"Student? Is there a problem?

"My name is Sara Luna—"

"Ah, ah, ah! In my class, you shall only be referred to as the Student and I as Mr. Bowen. Is that clear?"

Luna nodded before pulling herself up into the chair, her arm resting on the attached table.

"I have three rules in my class," Bowen cleared his throat. "If you follow them all, we'll get along splendidly. Rule number one: no phones are allowed in my classroom."

Luna looked around the cage, thinking her phone was with her. It wasn't.

"Rule number two," he continued, "there will be no eating or drinking allowed."

Is this man mad? Can't he see I'm locked up in a cage?

"And finally, rule number three—and this is the most important one of all—there will be no talking, especially when I'm speaking. If you have a question, you may raise your hand to be called upon."

Surely this guy can't be serious?

"Oh, and one more thing: I am very serious. Are there any questions before we begin?"

Luna raised her hand.

"Yes, Student. Go ahead."

"Why am I here?" she asked with a shaky voice.

He smiled. "This is a biology class. I think the answer is self-explanatory."

"You attacked me, brought me here, and locked me in this cage," she said in a loud voice.

"To be fair, how else would I ensure you would be on time for class today? Now, if there are no more questions, Student, we have a lot to cover, and I would like to get started."

Bowen retrieved a medical gown and gloves from the cabinet underneath the lab table and put them on. He then slipped large safety goggles over his glasses before walking over to the gurney and rolling it to the center of the room. Finally, he pulled the gray sheet off, revealing the nude body of a young Black woman.

Luna clamped her hand over her mouth, stifling her gasp as she recognized who it was. She'd seen her picture on the news. She'd been reported missing.

Bowen sorted through various medical instruments in a metal bin at the foot of the table as if a dead woman before him was nothing to be alarmed about. Unfortunately, the clanking of the stainless steel instruments pierced Luna's ears, causing tears to stream down her cheeks.

"Ah, found what I was looking for," Bowen said as he held up a scalpel in one hand. He adjusted his safety goggles before placing the sharp blade at the top of the woman's sternum. "Student, are you ready to begin?" He smiled at her and then proceeded to whistle as he made the first incision.

3

Sterling Gray was on a morning flight out of Dulles International Airport. A last-minute request from his supervisor had him scrambling to make the trip. He plopped down in the aisle seat in economy, an exit row. Gray couldn't stand having his legs folded up and the bureau wouldn't authorize business class for domestic flights. Exit rows were his only salvation.

Gray stretched his legs as he let out a breath. Sitting in the window seat was a man, probably in his late forties, with legs just as long as Gray's. Only, he was dressed in blue jeans and short-sleeved button-down—a contrast to the navy blue suit Gray wore.

"I can't stand sitting in the back." The man jabbed a thumb over his shoulder. "I always try to get into the exit row. It makes all the difference, don't it?"

"Definitely," Gray said.

"You visiting Iowa?" the man asked as he looked at Gray's suit.

"Yeah, I have a business meeting."

"Figures. Not too many people wear suits where I'm from. We keep it simple and comfortable."

Gray chuckled. "Nothing wrong with that."

"What sort of business you in? Irrigation? Cultivation? Fertilization?"

"No, no, no. Nothing farm related. I'm a federal agent."

The man pulled his head back in surprise. "You don't say. I never met an FBI person before. It *is* FBI, right? I know they got all kinds of agents with different acronyms . . . I think one is ATF."

"I work for the FBI."

"You catch the bad guys?"

"I do."

"Running and gunning all over the place, huh?"

"Not exactly. I work in the Behavioral Analysis Unit. I'm a profiler."

"Now, ain't that interesting? You gotta figure out them sickos. What's it like doing a job like that?"

"Honestly? I love it. I like figuring out the bad guy. The better we understand them, the easier it is to catch them. I love taking on cold cases that people think are unsolvable and solving them."

The man popped his eyebrows up. "Have you cracked any yet?"

"Sure. In fact, I just put a case to bed that was a decade old."

"You catch the guy?"

"We did."

"They probably need to make a movie about it. What's going on in Iowa? Must be serious to bring a guy like you out. Is it another cold case?"

"I can't comment on the nature of the investigation."

"Don't need to. I can already guess it's something serious. I imagine I'll read about it in the papers one day. My name's Leland Cook."

Gray took the man's hand and shook it. "Sterling Gray."

"Well, Agent Gray, I hope you catch your guy."

The United Airlines flight touched down at Des Moines International Airport a quarter past noon. Gray had flown in on the commuter flight from Washington, DC. at the request of the Ames Police Department. He was told Detectives Simon Sparks and Kenny Patton would be meeting him at the airport.

Gray didn't mind helping out local law enforcement with their investigations. Ever since he closed a cold case on a fugitive that had been dubbed the Penitent One, requests for Gray to lend his thinking to ongoing investigations had exploded. It kept him busy, but it also kept him on the road, monopolizing his personal time—something he was on the fence with.

With his carry-on bag rolling behind him, Gray walked out of the arrival hall to the curb outside. The hot, sticky air smacked him in the face, and his body started heating up under his suit. He removed a handkerchief from the inside of his jacket and dabbed at his forehead. His supervisor hadn't given him any other information except that two detectives would be picking him up. Typically, Gray would have made his own way, but the detectives had requested they met him there. A silver vehicle, a Crown Victoria, stopped right in front of him. The passenger window rolled down.

"Are you Special Agent Sterling Gray?" a smiling man asked. He had a bushy mustache, beady eyes, and looked to be in his midfifties.

"I am. You can drop the formalities with me. Sterling's fine."

"Welcome to Iowa. I'm Detective Sparks, and the guy driving is my partner, Detective Patton."

"How you doing?" Patton said, lowering his head so he could see Gray through the window. He was clean-cut and looked a lot younger than Sparks.

"Since we're moving to a first-name basis," Sparks said, "you can call me Simon, and he's Kenny." Sparks glanced at Gray's luggage. "If that's all you got, why don't you put it in the trunk, hop in the back, and we'll be on our way."

Gray stored the rolling carry-on in the trunk and climbed into the back seat.

"It may be the middle of September, but the leftover summer heat is still broiling our skins," Sparks said. "Normally, we dress up in fancy suits like you have on, but when it's hot like this, we prefer jeans and a polo shirt, so feel free to dress down. No one here will judge you for it."

"I might just do that," Gray said as he loosened his tie a bit.

"We appreciate you coming out here on such short notice," Patton said as he looked at Gray in the rearview mirror. "To be honest, we didn't think the FBI would bother."

"Well, the FBI did bother, and I'm here to assist with all the resources the Bureau has to offer."

"Any reason why they flew you in instead of assigning someone from the local office in Des Moines?" Sparks asked.

"I work in the Behavioral Analysis Unit based in Quantico. My background is better suited for your investigation."

"Is that so? So you come to help us simple folks solve crime?" Sparks said.

Gray ignored the dig. "I'm simply here to assist."

"You deal with the sickos, right?" Patton asked as he made a left at the light. "That's all I need to know, because that's what we got on our hands. How many of these guys have you brought down?"

"If you're talking chased and cuffed, very few. My specialty, in a nutshell, is figuring out how they think and trying to interpret their next move. I read your report on the flight over here. This is exactly the type of investigation I should be involved with. There's nothing ordinary about how the victim was killed."

"Kenny and I have worked in law enforcement most of our lives," Sparks said. "Neither of us have seen anything like this before, but I ain't never met a criminal that could outsmart me yet. It's just a matter of time before we get him."

"Like I said earlier, I'm here to assist you. I'll do my best."

"You ever visit Iowa before?" Sparks asked.

"Des Moines, yes. Ames, no. In fact, I've never heard of it."

"Ames is a small town about forty-five minutes north of Des Moines," Sparks continued as he turned up the AC. "We have a population of about sixty thousand people, half of which is students at ISU. We're a small community. Everyone knows everyone. The university started back in session in August, so the town is at full capacity."

"I looked up the crimes statistics for Ames—not a lot of violent crime for the population. So what you have here is sort of an anomaly."

"You're right about that. Most of the crime in the area is petty and connected with the university. We do have a gang presence, and every now and then, we'll have a body drop because of that. There's a lot of property crime, but overall, Ames is a pretty safe place to live. I'll be honest, when that first body appeared, it put the town on edge. When word got out about the second one, people started making a ruckus at the town hall, demanding we find the person responsible. I know there's a train of thought that says you need a minimum of three bodies to even use the serial killer label, but my gut started screaming when that second body hit. And usually, it ain't wrong."

"Well, I'm glad you guys pushed for the FBI's involvement."

"We didn't. Our bosses did," Sparks said.

"We thought we'd drive you straight to the most recent crime scene, if you're all right with that," Patton said.

"No better time than the present."

A little while later, the passing homes outside Gray's window turned into passing cornfields as far as he could see. Patton slowed and made a right turn onto a dirt road that led into one of the fields. The cornstalks towered eight feet high on both sides of the car, cutting off visibility other than the dirt road. A gentle breeze fluttered the wispy tassels at the top of the stalks as Gray noted the bright green ears.

"I can tell you like corn," Patton asked.

Gray crinkled his brow. "Oh, yeah? Why is that?"

"Because you're a little husky." Patton and Sparks chuckled. "Sorry, it's not often we get a chance to tell our corny jokes to outsiders."

"Don't worry, I'm all ears."

Patton brought the car to a stop.

Sparks pointed down a row of cornstalks. "The second body was found up ahead by a bunch of kids playing hide-and-go-seek. If it weren't for them, that body wouldn't have been found until harvest time. The first body was discovered a couple miles down the highway just off the side of the road—son of a bitch didn't even try to hide it. Just tossed it to the side like a bag of trash."

Patton set the parking brake, and the three men climbed out.

"Has CSI finished conducting their portion of the investigation?" Gray asked as he followed Sparks down a row of cornstalks.

"Just yesterday. That's why it wasn't in your report. I'll give you the rundown now: The killer parked his car on the same road we drove in on. Too many tire tracks to pin one down to a particular vehicle. CSI pulled DNA in the next row over, so our guy dragged the victim from his vehicle through that row until he reached a spot up ahead. She was already dead."

They came into a small clearing where the cornstalks had been cut away.

"Did the killer clear this area, or was it cleared by CSI?" Gray asked.

"They did it after the body was removed. She was found right there, nude, lying on her back. She had stitches running from the top of her sternum to her pubic bone. We met with the medical examiner this morning. The victim's innards were removed with a sharp instrument. Scalpel, most likely. They were then packed into a plastic bag and sealed before being stuffed back into the cavity and the incision sewed back up."

"'Lesson two' was written on the outside of the bag," Patton said. "Exact same thing had been done to the first victim, except that bag had 'lesson one' written on it. So he's trying to teach us a lesson. That's what he's trying to do. I mean, that's what these guys do: They taunt, right?"

"It's possible," Gray said.

"You have any initial thoughts on why the hell someone would do that to someone . . . remove their innards only to put it back in them like a stuffed turkey?" Sparks asked.

"Not at the moment. What can you tell me about this victim?"

Sparks shoved both hands into his pant pockets. "Her name was Sofia Garcia. She's from out of state and was a junior at ISU." He turned to Patton. "You recall where she was from?"

"I think she was from Oklahoma . . . Tulsa, I believe."

"She lived off campus in her own apartment. No signs of a break-in there. CSI combed the place and could only find traces of her DNA. She was last seen studying at the library on campus. Body was discovered three days later. The medical examiner placed her time of death about eight to ten hours before the body was discovered."

"So he kept her alive for a couple days."

Sparks nodded. "It's the same story with the first victim as well. Sheila Wang was a senior at ISU, also lived off campus in her own housing. She was reported missing by her boyfriend. We already cleared him. Her body was found three days later up the highway."

"So both victims were female, attending ISU, and living off campus. Our killer kept them alive for three days before killing them and bringing their bodies to the cornfields."

"The first victim, Wang, was Chinese. Garcia, well, she was Mexican," Patton said. "A few days ago, Nia Carter was reported as missing. She was Black and lived off campus. If the three-day window is right, we're just about out of time with her."

Gray ran his hand through his hair. "Okay, that puts us on the clock. So, possibly targeting women of color; all students at ISU, living off campus . . . Anything else to connect these three women?"

Sparks shook his head. "They all ran in different circles; didn't share any classes. They came from normal middle-class families, from what we can tell. No previous arrest records. Wang was studying engineering, Garcia was studying business. The missing girl, Carter, was studying political science."

"Well, it's clear the killer familiarized himself with their routines before grabbing them," Gray said. "This isn't opportunistic. He definitely has a type."

"We interviewed all their friends, the faculty that interacted with them, and came up with nothing concrete," Patton added.

Gray rested his hands on his hips. "Do you think it's someone who might just be familiar with the university, you know, like a person who makes deliveries to the cafeteria every week or an off-site contractor?"

"Could be. We haven't explored that road because nothing we learned so far had pointed us that way. I mean, if we consider that, it widens the pool of possibilities. But the way we see it now, it's most likely another student. They know the campus, they know the routines of other students, they blend," Sparks said. "It's harder for an outsider, like yourself, to come in and not be noticed."

Just then, Patton's phone rang.

"Patton here. Yeah, we're with him right now. I see. Okay." Patton shook his head as he disconnected the call. "Another student was just reported missing. It might be our guy striking again."

4

Patton stepped on the gas pedal, and the cruiser sped east on Highway 30 toward Ames. "The university is located in the center of town," he said, "about ten minutes away."

"Earlier, you mentioned the student body makes up half the population of Ames," Gray said. "I imagine everything in Ames revolves around the university."

"It's the lifeline of the town," Sparks said. "Has been since it was founded in 1858. When I spoke earlier about the complaints after the second body popped up, I was referring to the alumni. They're very powerful. In short, they run Ames. In fact, our esteemed governor is an alumnus. Even Kenny here is a fine graduate."

"Are you an alumnus as well?" Gray asked Sparks.

"Nah, I'm a Husker all the way, but after I graduated from the University of Nebraska, I met a gal from Ames. I've been here ever since." Sparks shifted in his seat so he could look over his shoulder at Gray. "A lot of important people are looking to us to fix this mess. I ain't never let them down before."

"We don't have a lot of time before Nia Carter turns into a homicide," Gray said. "The one saving grace is that our guy is moving fast. That can lead to mistakes on his part."

"That's what we're hoping for," Sparks said. "Two bodies and two missing persons since ISU came back into session. It's a lot in a short amount of time. You think that means anything?"

"My first thought is impatience. He's eager to make a point fast and possibly in a big way. He doesn't want his actions swept under the rug. It's important that he doesn't feel like he's being ignored."

"Could it just be about attention from the media?" Patton asked. "Nowadays, everyone is craving their limelight in social media by doing or saying anything that will get them views or likes."

"It's possible, but if that were the case, he'd be posting on social media. I didn't see any evidence of that in the report. Was something like that left out?"

Patton shook his head. "There is none."

"It's likely some other motivator driving him to move quickly. It's uncommon. Contract killers for the Mexican cartel move at that pace, not serial killers."

Both Patton's and Sparks's phones chimed.

"The latest missing-person report just came through," Sparks said. "Here's what we know so far: The missing girl's name is Sara Luna, eighteen years old and a sophomore at ISU. She's studying psychology. She *does* live on campus at Friley Hall. I know it. It's on the western end of the campus and the one hall that doesn't allow alcohol or drugs. It's not party central. If she was taken by our guy, then he has no preference if they're living on campus or off campus. In my head, that points to a student." Sparks turned around to look at Gray. "You disagree?"

"Not necessarily. But I would say his actions convey confidence. Also, something else could be prompting him to pick up the pace. Do you know if any of the other women were party people—outgoing and sociable? Or were they more studious, quiet types?"

"I don't think we got a read one way or another," Sparks said. "Says here the roommate filed the missing-person report a few hours ago. We'll see what she has to say."

Patton merged off the highway and onto Lincoln Way, a three-lane motorway cutting through Ames. Looking outside his window, Gray couldn't help noticing that the place looked more like the suburbs than a city. There were plenty of trees and open areas with manicured lawns. To add to that, more and more homes along the road were springing up, and then the three lanes were reduced to two lanes. For some reason, he had it in his head that it would be more urban with such a large student body population—something with an edge.

"Doesn't look like a university town," Gray said.

"No, it doesn't," Sparks said. "The university and the surrounding area were purposely built to be that way—a lot of green. It's an open campus. The buildings are on the outside, and in the center is a large grassy field. I bet you didn't even realize we're driving past the university right now," Sparks said. "It's on the left."

"I honestly thought it was a park," Gray said surprisingly. "That makes it easy to move around the area and not be noticed. It'll make catching this guy that much harder."

Patton made a left onto Welch Road, and a few yards farther turned left into a small parking lot next to a four-story redbrick building. The three men exited the vehicle and made their way to the entrance of Friley Hall.

"Hey, for now it might be good to let Kenny and I lead with the questions," Sparks said on the walk over. "We're not territorial, but this is our backyard . . . At least until you get all caught up and stuff."

"No problem," Gray said. "If I have something to add, I'll chime in."

Just inside the door was a reception counter with a student staffing it.

"Hello. I'm Detective Sparks. This is Detective Patton and Special Agent Gray. We need to speak to Candace Stevens."

"Oh, crap," the young woman said. "This is serious. We had heard that Sara might be missing—she's Candace's roommate. Do you think the same thing has happened to her? I mean, the same guy took her?"

"What makes you think it's a he?" Gray asked.

"Oh, uh, I dunno. I was just saying that to mean 'someone.'"

Gray continued with his questions. "How well do you know Ms. Luna?"

"Not that well. She's a sophomore. I mean, I see her around. I know who she is, but we're not, like, friends or anything like that. She's a bit on the quiet side."

"Is there a way for you to contact Ms. Stevens for us?" Sparks interrupted. "We'd appreciate it."

"Yeah, sure." She tapped her fingers on the laptop in front of her. "I just need to locate her number on the hall registry." The girl made a quick call on her phone. "She'll be right down. Feel free to wait over there if you want." She pointed to an area where there were chairs.

Ten minutes later, a young woman with brown hair pulled up into a messy bun appeared. She wore Iowa State University sweatpants and an oversize hoodie.

"Ms. Stevens. We appreciate you meeting with us." Sparks made the quick introductions and then asked if they could look at Luna's side of the room while they spoke. Stevens agreed and led the men back up to her room on the fourth floor.

Sparks cleared his throat. "Ms. Stevens—"

"You can call me Candace," she said.

"Candace, can you tell us how you came to think Sara was missing?"

They all squeezed into the elevator, and Candace used her key card to access the floor.

"Well, she always studies late at the library. She's super serious about school. Anyway, she didn't come back around the usual time. I tend to study in the room, so I know when she comes back. I figured she got held up with something else. I wasn't concerned or anything until this morning when I woke at seven. She wasn't in her bed."

The elevator doors opened, and they exited.

"Is there a chance she could have come back to the room and then left without your realizing it?" Patton asked as they followed Candace down the hallway, passing numerous closed doors.

"No way. I'm a light sleeper. I would have heard her."

"But you were positive Sara went to the library last night?"

"Not one hundred percent. I last saw Sara in the afternoon around three. Then I left to meet up with some friends. When I got back at seven, she was gone, so I assumed she went to the library." Candace stopped outside a door. "This is our room." She used her key card to unlock it and led the way in.

The room was compact. It had bunk beds, two desks with chairs, two wardrobe closets, and dressers. There was a small refrigerator tucked between the desks. Clothes were strewn across one of the chairs and across the bottom bed. Candace quickly kicked a bra that was on the floor under the bed.

"Sorry about the mess. The Korean boy-band poster is mine. I'm crazy about them. Sara sleeps on the top bunk. So you can see I obviously would have known if she came back. Everything on this side of the room is hers."

There weren't a ton of personal items. A couple family photos tacked up on a cork bulletin board above her desk, but nothing with Luna and friends. Standard toiletries lined the top of her dresser. Patton opened her wardrobe closet. Nothing out of the ordinary jumped out.

"Would you consider yourself close friends with Sara?" Sparks turned to face Candace.

"This is the first time we're rooming together, so we just met. I mean, I've seen her around before, but I didn't really know her until this year. We get along okay."

Sparks nodded. "Do you know who her other friends are?"

"I know some people she talks to, but I think their interaction is mostly because of a class assignment or they're part of a study group. She's kind of an introvert. And like I said before, she's pretty serious about her studies."

"What about family? Did you get the sense she was close with them?"

"Normal like most people, I guess. I hear her on the phone with them."

"I don't see a bookbag or a purse around her desk," Patton said.

"Sara doesn't really use a purse, just a backpack, and she takes it everywhere."

"Excuse me, Candace," Gray inserted. "How far of a walk is it from Friley Hall to the library?"

"The Parks Library isn't far from here, maybe a ten-minute walk at the most."

"I'm assuming the pathway is lit at night?"

"For the most part, yeah. Depends on which way you walk."

"Can you see it from your window?" Gray asked.

"Not really." Candace opened the window and leaned out a bit. "You see that water tower over there?"

Gray looked over Candace's shoulder. "Yeah, I see it."

"The Parks Library is just to the right of that. Unfortunately, that other building is blocking it. But you can see it's not that far."

"No, it isn't, and the walkway heading in that direction looks pretty direct."

"Yeah, it's not spooky to walk around campus at night, if that's what you're thinking, and plus, there are usually people out at all hours."

"Do you know if Ms. Luna was meeting a study group at the library last night?" Gray asked.

"She didn't say. She mentioned that she likes to go into the private study rooms on the second floor."

Gray looked back at Sparks and Patton, indicating he had nothing more to ask Candace.

"We appreciate your time, Candace," Sparks said. He handed her his business card. "If you can think of anything else that might be of importance, my direct cell number is on there."

On the way out of Friley Hall, Sparks turned to Gray. "How are you holding up? You okay to keep going? I don't know if you're the type to get jet-lagged. If you need to take a moment at your hotel, it's all right with us. We'll keep moving and catch you up later."

"Time is not our friend at the moment. Right now, Luna's alive and breathing, and she's counting on us to keep it that way." Gray pointed to the CCTV cameras mounted at the entrance. "We need to pull the footage from those cameras and see if we can establish a timeline."

"Noted," Patton said.

Sparks pointed to a pathway. "That's the way to the library."

5

Gray walked out in front of the two detectives, preferring to take in the surroundings without commentary from Sparks. Since leaving Friley Hall, he'd been pointing out potential areas of interest where an attack could be made. As much as Gray thought the hiding places Sparks was noting were worth exploring, his observations began to paint a different picture.

During the day, an abundance of students crisscrossed the campus—night would be the best time for abduction. The pathways were out in the open, with multiple lampposts along the way. The campus didn't look car-friendly. Whoever took Luna needed to have a car nearby. Dragging or carrying an unconscious person across campus without being seen would have been hard to do, even at night.

One question kept rising to the top of Gray's thoughts. What if Luna wasn't abducted on campus? Maybe she wasn't as studious as everyone was led to believe. Perhaps she wasn't even at the library the previous night. However, if she had been taken from campus during her walk back to her room, it was possible she knew her abductor and had let her guard down, making it easier to get her into a nearby vehicle.

Gray knew that was only scratching the surface, though. The key to catching this killer was figuring out who he was. He had bit his tongue since meeting Sparks and Patton, wanting to see their approach to the investigation. They were handling it like any detective would, and Gray was fine to have them do that. But that's not why he was there. He wasn't an extra hand, there to compile evidence and leads. His job was to bring the killer to life, to put a face on a ghost.

One thing in particular stood out to Gray when he looked over the crime scene photos. The stitching used to sew up the incisions was crudely done—amateurish at best. This person wasn't involved with the medical profession. Nor did Gray get the feeling that it was a hunter or even someone with taxidermy experience. This was someone who watched a bunch of YouTube videos and then went to work. He had no hard evidence to prove his theory, but his gut had never steered him wrong, and he was willing to go along and see where it took him.

Gray also wasn't entirely sure if the same thoughtlessness was put into removing the victim's insides. That detail wasn't in the report. Were they ripped out like one was cutting a fish, or were they carefully and precisely removed as if they were being saved for organ donation?

If Gray's instincts were leading him down the right path, then a picture of the killer was being formed. He might have been pretending to be someone he wasn't. And if that were true, then the role he was playing would be the driving factor, not the actual kill. Gray made a note of three things that could be motivating the killer:

- *Making a point.*
- *Role-playing.*
- *Under pressure—timing.*

"I see a lot of students walking around," Gray said. "This pathway is out in the open. There are lampposts. I've seen a couple of places where someone could hide and jump out, but whoever took Luna needed a vehicle nearby, and this campus isn't car friendly."

"I see what you're saying," Sparks said. "We're out in the open. Someone would have seen something. But if our guy is a student, no one would blink an eye."

"Does the university have their own campus police?" Gray asked.

"You're looking at it. Part of the Ames Police Department's jurisdiction is the campus."

"So there are regular patrols during the day and night."

"That's right. I know what you're getting at. Luna started off as a missing-person case, not a homicide, but we all know where it's most likely heading. As soon as we get back to the station, we'll talk to the officers who originally filed the report, and we'll also find out who was on patrol last night. We might be able to glean more information from them."

A few minutes later, the pathway led the men to a lush green field. At the opposite end was a cream-colored building with a modern design that resembled Getty architecture.

"That fancy building over there is the Parks Library," Sparks said. "We're familiar with most of the faculty here."

As they crossed the field, Gray noted that if Luna had been abducted after leaving the library, this was where it most likely had happened. Many trees dotted the area, and the pathways that crossed the field didn't have lampposts. To the right, Gray spied a road that looked like it ran along the field; a vehicle could have been parked there. But still, the distance, about thirty yards, was problematic. There were several routes Luna could have taken back to her room. It was possible.

"Are you familiar with these other buildings?" Gray asked.

"Classrooms, mostly," Sparks answered.

"So they're closed at night," Gray said. "Only students utilizing the library would have a need to be in this area. There's tree coverage, and the road just beyond those trees could be used for a getaway depending on how vacant this place becomes at night."

"If she cut through that thicket of trees over there to walk along the road, it's a quick snatch-and-grab," Patton answered. "But it's not the most direct path back to her dorm. The perimeter of the library building has security cameras installed. We'll have the footage pulled and see what comes of it."

Gray brought up the rear as they entered the library. Sitting at the reception desk were a couple of student staff members. Gray looked around, and the library seemed busy with students. The library's center had an atrium, which allowed him to see the second and third floors. He spotted what looked like the study rooms that Luna was fond of. Sparks produced his identification and had a short conversation, but Gray was too far away to make out what the whispers were about.

"We're friendly with the head librarian here, Ruth Hampton," Sparks said after approaching Gray. "We'll get the ball rolling with her, see if we can connect all four girls to the library."

A few minutes later, a woman who appeared to be in her late fifties, maybe early sixties, approached them. She was dressed in a jacket and matching skirt and had a pleasant smile on her face.

"Simon, Kenny, this is a nice surprise. What brings you here?"

"Hello, Ruth," Sparks said. "Sorry to barge in on you like this, but we need to have a short conversation. Is there a place we can talk privately?"

"Oh, oh. This doesn't sound good."

Sparks cracked a smile as he put up his hands. "You're not in trouble, nor is any of your staff. We just have a few questions."

Hampton led the men back to a small conference room on the first floor.

"It'll be much more comfortable in here than my cramped office," she said. Hampton looked directly at Gray. "I don't believe I've seen you around before."

"This is Special Agent Gray. He's helping us with an investigation."

"Well, I have a pretty good idea which one. I'm glad the FBI is here. Whoever did that to those two young girls deserves to be castrated and turned into pig feed. Sorry about my words. Every time I think about what happened, it makes my blood boil. How can I be of help?"

"Do you know a student named Sara Luna?"

Hampton clasped her hand across her mouth. "Please don't tell me there's another one. So that's two more missing?"

"She was reported missing earlier this morning by her roommate. She was said to have been here last night."

Patton pulled up a photo of Luna and handed his phone over to Hampton.

"Oh yes, I've seen this girl practically every day since the school year resumed. I don't know her personally, though."

"Do you recall seeing her last night? She likes to sit in the private study rooms."

"I wasn't here last night, but I can check with the staff that was on hand. Could you email me the picture?" Hampton typed her email address into Patton's phone.

"What about the other girls?" Sparks produced photos of the two victims and the missing person. "Do you recall seeing them coming in the library a lot?"

"Now that you mention it, the first girl was in here quite a bit as well. I'm not positive about the second one. It's early in the school year, and things are always crazy. I'm usually stuck in meetings. But the other missing girl, Nia Carter. I know her. She's in here a lot."

"Ms. Hampton—" Gray started.

"Please, call me Ruth."

"Ruth, are only students and faculty allowed in here, or is the general public free to come inside?"

"The library is open to the public. All print and electronic materials can be used freely on-site. However, there are restrictions in regards to borrowing material."

"So anyone in Ames or even outside of Ames can visit during the day and night."

"That's correct."

"And do they need to register or leave an ID if they're not a student or a faculty member?"

"The only time we require identification is when someone wants to borrow material. And in that case, only students and alumni, or faculty, retired or current, are afforded those privileges. So what are you getting at, Agent Gray? Do you think the person responsible is associated with ISU?"

"Quite the opposite. I think this person has nothing to do with the university but wishes he had."

6

Luna sat against the rear of the cage, her knees drawn up against her chest and arms wrapped around them. She had been forced to watch Bowen dissect that woman on the table like she was a frog in a biology class.

He had continually asked her if she had any questions, even becoming annoyed when she didn't. So much so that she had begun to fabricate questions just to keep him calm. But the strangest thing about the entire ordeal was that Bowen didn't appear to know what he was talking about. He guessed at specific body parts. He would remove something and quickly put it back, stating he had gotten the order of removal wrong. He was very impatient, constantly berating himself under his breath. Luna got the impression that he was doing his best to pretend to be a professor of biology but, in fact, was inept.

But his qualifications were the least of her worries. Luna couldn't help but wonder if she was the next lesson for someone else. After Bowen had completed his faux dissection, he told her class was over, assigned her homework, which was weird because she didn't even have a pen and paper to write on. Before leaving, he put a small training toilet into the kennel, the ones used for toddlers.

That was roughly five hours ago if the clock hanging on the wall was correct. The time was either a little after one in the afternoon or one at night. She couldn't be sure. Bowen hadn't returned since, and she hadn't heard any noise outside the door.

Luna pulled on the padlock on the cage door, but it was securely locked. The cage wasn't made entirely of iron bars, just the frame. The rest of the cell was wired mesh. Luna imagined she could easily lift it up and crawl out from under it if it weren't bolted into the floor.

She was hungry—thirsty, more than anything. Bowen hadn't offered food or water when he was there. Maybe it was his way to enforce his stupid rule about not eating or drinking during class. But the class was over, so the rules didn't apply.

"Hello!" Luna called out. "Mr. Bowen? Are you there?"

She waited a few moments for an answer, but none came.

"Mr. Bowen!" She shouted a little louder. "I'm thirsty. Can I please have some water? Please!"

Upstairs, Bowen sat on the leather recliner in his living room, sipping grape soda while playing a mobile video game. The game challenged him to build a university and attract students. Bowen spent hours maintaining his university by adding value, like a better library or expanding the athletic field to a dome stadium. He kept the students happy and increased enrollment, which made him more money.

Bowen had always thought he would make a great dean of students. He, of course, had no professional qualifications, just his own time spent attending school. He managed a year of community college before being disillusioned with how the school was managed and their treatment of the students. It felt like all the school cared about was money. Bowen wasn't against profit, but there was no real value being returned. *What's so damn hard about teaching a student something? I simply don't get it. I've managed great success in only a short amount of time. Why on earth can't these educators do the same? Sadly, as the case always is, one must lead by example.*

"Mr. Bowen!" a voice called out.

Bowen supposed he heard the yelling in the back of his mind, but he was too involved with constructing an Olympic-size swimming pool for his university. He paid no attention and continued to build and dream about his success. He had also started thinking about his next student. He had a few lucky ones in mind, ones he'd been keeping an eye on and that seemed worthy of what he had to offer.

"Please, Mr. Bowen!" the voice called out once more.

That last time he couldn't ignore it. *What is it with this student? Doesn't she know class is over? I have a life too.*

"Mr. Bowen. Can I please have something to drink?"

Bowen put his phone down on the coffee table in front of him and went to his kitchen to fetch a bottle of water before heading downstairs.

The door opened and in walked Bowen. "Student. You're disturbing me while I'm involved in some very important matters."

"I'm sorry, it's just that I'm so thirsty."

He walked over to the cage, unlocked the padlock with a key he kept in his pants pocket. "Here you go," he said as he handed her the water.

Luna quickly unscrewed the cap and gulped down the water, finishing it all at once.

"Thank you," she said as she caught her breath. "I'm really sorry about disturbing you."

"It's fine so long as it doesn't become a habit."

"Then maybe you can bring me another bottle of water now, you know, so I can drink it later."

Bowen let out a long breath as he rolled his eyes. "I guess I can do that." He closed the cage door and locked it. "I'll be right back."

"Excuse me, Mr. Bowen. I have a question."

"Sure, what is it?"

"Will we be having another class soon?"

Bowne cocked his head to the side. "You want another class?"

"Yes, I found the last one very interesting."

A smile formed on Bowen's face as he took a few steps back to the cage. "Now you have my curiosity tickled. What is it that you found interesting?"

"If I had to put it in words, I'd say it was the simplicity in which you conducted the lesson. It was so easy to follow. And you didn't spend time on boring details. I got a lot out of it. I learned things."

"Well, Student, hearing you say this makes me very happy. I've always thought most educators made the job harder than it should be, resulting in the student not learning. I'm very pleased to hear you say this. Let me give it some thought."

Luna watched Bowen until he disappeared behind the closed door. That was the second time he had opened the cage door without worry or caution, and she wondered if, just maybe, that could be turned into an opportunity.

The gurney had been pushed back against the wall. She knew the medical instruments were in the metal container under the sheet. She knew for sure there was a scalpel and a metal hammer because she had seen him use them both. If she could slip by Bowen when he opened the cage door and get to the gurney, she'd have a weapon to fight him off and escape.

She waited patiently for Bowen to return.

Ten minutes passed.

Fifteen minutes.

Thirty.

But he hadn't returned.

How much time does this idiot need to get a bottle of water?

While waiting, she imagined the different ways her escape might play out.

He opens the door and I rush out, pushing him back onto his butt. Some quick steps later, I'm at the gurney with a scalpel in my hand. Or I scream really loud and swing my arms around like a crazy woman, clawing at his face. That would also catch him off guard, and I can slip past easily.

Of course, the scenarios that entered her head after wasn't encouraging.

What if my screaming and clawing at his face doesn't faze him? What if, instead, he easily pushes me back into the cage and locks it? Or what if I'm not fast enough, and he tackles me from behind and slams my face into the floor, beating it to a bloody pulp? Or worse, I can't find the scalpel in time, and he catches up with me, and while punching my face, finds the scalpel and slices me up? He'll know what I said earlier about his lesson was bullshit. No. Stop it. You can't think this way. Be positive. Keep him believing he's doing an incredible job. He'll lower his guard.

As time wore on, it became clear that Bowen wasn't returning anytime soon. Luna would have to wait for her opportunity.

7

Patton held the door open, allowing Gray and Sparks to exit the library first.

"We can add Parks Library to the list of things the victims have in common," Sparks said as he hiked up his jeans.

"This is definitely where he's hunting," Patton added. "I'm hoping we get lucky with the security footage."

"Sterling, we got a lot of things we can start running down," Sparks said. "How about we drop you back off at your hotel? You can do what you need to do, and we can reconvene tomorrow or later tonight if something promising rises to the surface. Or, if you want, you're welcome to pop over to the station, if that helps move things along."

Gray nodded. "I'd like some time alone with what we learned today. I'll connect with you guys later tonight."

Sparks and Patton dropped Gray off at his hotel, only a five-minute drive from the ISU campus. After checking in, he ordered room service and settled in behind his laptop. He was eager to get his thoughts down and start his initial report for his supervisor.

In Gray's mind, he already believed Nia Carter, reported missing a few days ago was dead. His focus was on Sara Luna—he had a real chance at saving her. He didn't want her blood on his hands.

As Gray organized his thoughts both in his mind and on his laptop, one obvious thing stood out to him about the investigation: body mutilation. While pieces of the victim were removed, they weren't discarded. A body part pinned to a wall could be a message. A body part shoved down the victim's throat could convey anger. What was this guy trying to say by removing and then replacing the victim's insides back where they were taken from? And in a bag?

It certainly wasn't out of sexual gratification. No foreign DNA was discovered on the victims, and there were no signs of sexual assault. Gray also didn't note anything that led him to believe the killer was being told to kill. He was no Son of Sam, listening to voices in his head. Those types of killers tended to leave messages or signs behind. Was bagging the innards and sewing them back up a sign? Gray didn't believe so. It meant something, but it wasn't necessarily trying to communicate. It could just be as simple as cleaning up to make the disposal of the body more efficient.

Now, this didn't mean there wasn't anger involved. The killer was most likely acting out of frustration. And if that was the case, then he might believe he was righting a wrong. He would need to be focused and mission-oriented. A killer like this operated much like someone keen to cross off items on a to-do list. There is an end goal.

It could also start to explain the speed at which he's abducting and killing his victims. The one hiccup was that he kept them alive. Did he need to do something during that time? Was it essential? Was it something specific to the victims?

All four women were students. Gray assumed that was the one steadfast requirement. All four women could be placed at the library. Two were there a lot. The other two had to be as well. The school has only been in session for a short time. How else would the killer know? He's in the library as much as they are. Another student? Faculty? Cleaning staff? Or is it someone from the general public, someone who might consider himself to be an intellectual?

There was no question the killer was male, between the ages of eighteen and twenty-five. He would be white and most likely have a superiority complex. Selecting victims from the library pool could mean he's looking for others like himself or those that have the potential to be like him: above others.

A knock on the door pulled Gray out of his thoughts: room service. He had ordered a double bacon cheeseburger with fries and a cherry Coke to wash it down. As soon as he tipped the guy and ushered him out the door, Gray attacked the burger. He hadn't eaten all day, and the savory meat tasted like heaven. Gray took a moment to relax and enjoy his food rather than work and eat simultaneously, which was often the case.

A little guilt bubbled up in his throat as thoughts of Luna snuck into his mind. Was she being fed or given water? Was she conscious? Thinking just a tiny bit about that was enough to damper Gray's appetite. He finished his burger and most of the fries before sitting back down in front of his laptop.

Gray already had the basis of a profile for their killer. It was a pretty standard issue.

- *Unsub is a white male with a superiority complex.*
- *Educated but arrogant.*
- *His kills are mission-oriented—he wants to make a point.*
- *He believes what he's doing is important.*
- *He questions or challenges the competence of authority.*
- *Body mutilation is a statement or an example.*
- *Familiar with Ames; most likely a local.*
- *He's young-looking and blends easily with other students.*

Gray leaned back in the leather executive chair as he stared at the profile. There was something off. He knew he was right about classifying him as mission-oriented. He wanted to get rid of something he perceived to be wrong. But he considered himself an intellectual. Why get rid of other intellectuals? The victims he had targeted weren't party animals. The first two victims studied hard and didn't appear to be slackers. Luna lived in a residence hall that was the furthest thing from a party scene. What was it that they did that came across as something wrong?

Was this nothing more than a racially motivated attack? Not really. Luna was white, or at least looked white. Age wasn't a factor. Gray didn't even consider it being financially motivated because of the middle-class backgrounds. So why set out to abduct and kill these women? If it wasn't about them, then what was it about? Were they just a conduit to prove a point that had nothing to do with them?

Gray paced his room as he gave that question thought, eventually stopping to stare out his window. He had a room on the third floor, and the window faced the parking lot in front of the hotel.

There was one other thought that Gray had yet to fully dive into, but it was instinctually the first thing that came to mind when he had been questioning Hampton earlier: that the killer wasn't associated with the university but wishes he had been. It wasn't anything she said, per se, that triggered the thought, but it made Gray think whether it could be an alumnus angered by something the school had done in the past. Or even a young man who wanted nothing more than to attend ISU but wasn't accepted. Could that be the real motivator?

8

It was seven p.m. when Bowen arrived at the ISU campus. It took forty-five minutes for him to walk the distance from his place—a simple straight shot along Lincoln Way. Sometimes he took the bus, but he'd usually walk as it helped him sort through his thoughts. The only time he ever drove to the campus was when he was absolutely sure he was picking up a new student. That night he intended to narrow his selections down.

When Bowen reached the campus, he headed in along Welch Road and then walked along one of the many pathways crossing the campus. The sun had set by then, and the lampposts glowed. They weren't terribly bright. Just a tiny area directly underneath each was lit. Bowen always felt they acted like markers dotting the way forward. They were definitely more for aesthetics than safety.

His attire was nothing like what he wore when he was conducting a class. He dressed normal, in a black hoodie and jeans with tears at the knees. On his head, he had a worn ball cap. He always had his earbuds on and a backpack hanging off his back. He looked like any other student at ISU.

Bowen entered the Parks Library and made the usual circle around the first floor, getting a quick overview of who was there. He saw a lot of familiar faces, but none of them were suitable for his cause. He already had two singled out. They were consistent with their nightly appearances and studied alone. He wasn't interested in ones that came to the library to socialize with others. The ones that caught his eye were quiet, kept to themselves, weren't always on their phone messaging or shopping. He didn't see his two favorites, so he headed up to the second floor and walked past the private study rooms. One by one, he peeked through a small door window, but they didn't seem to be there, either. *That's strange.*

He proceeded to walk down every aisle, thinking they could be looking for a book, but he didn't see them. He had one more floor to check, but in all of his time in watching them, not once had he seen them visit the third floor.

Alas, Bowen trudged up the steps and searched the entire third floor. He came up empty. He glanced at his watch. *They should've been here by now. Maybe they'll show up a little later.*

Bowen had wavered on whether to drive to the library that night. He was eager to move on to the next lesson plan but felt like he needed to watch the two once more before selecting one to be his next student. In hindsight, he should have driven if he did choose one and the opportunity to take her presented itself. But he already knew both of these women lived in on-campus housing. That presented challenges.

His first student, Sheila Wang, was quickly taken outside her apartment building. His second student, Sofia Garcia, posed no real challenge either. She always walked to and from the library from her apartment. The student he cut up that morning, Nia Carter, well, she actually thought Bowen was cute and accepted an invitation to go back to his place.

With his current student, Sara Luna, Bowen had gotten lucky as she had decided not to head back to her residence hall after finishing up at the library. He took her after she exited a convenience store, which was a blessing because he was a little skeptical of taking her since she lived on campus.

As Bowen left the third floor, he'd begun thinking of Luna's comment to him, or rather, her compliment. None of his other students had recognized his efforts. If anything, they complained or ignored him. Not Luna, though. She seemed different. And that prompted him to seriously consider another lesson. Could she be the one student who actually understood his plight?

Bowen was well aware that he couldn't change the way schools operated, but he could punish. First, he would demonstrate that anyone could teach if they weren't blinded by greed. Secondly, he would take away promising students who excelled in a system designed to take their money with very little thought toward their education. But if he gave Luna another lesson, he'd be ignoring the syllabus for his own class.

Was that a bad thing? Maybe Sara understood how horrible the education at ISU was. But, clearly, she saw the incredible difference he had made after one class. It only confirmed that his efforts were worthy. Maybe a student like Sara deserved more of what he had to offer.

Bowen headed back to the first floor, after which he spotted the two women he had chosen as potential students. They were sitting at the communal tables in the atrium. Bowen sat at the same table and removed his laptop from his backpack. *So, now, which one of you will be the lucky one?*

9

Gray had been working on the profile nonstop since checking into his room. He felt reasonably good about where he had landed and was ready to share his findings with Sparks and Patton. After a quick shower to revitalize his body and mind, he sent Sparks and Patton a message that he was on his way. When he arrived at the two-story redbrick building, he found Patton waiting for him outside.

"Sterling, I see you took our advice on the dress code."

"Hey, you know, when in Rome . . ."

Gray had changed into jeans and button-down that was tucked in. He had a light jacket on to conceal his hip holster. He really had felt out of place in the suit earlier in the day.

"Anything new to convey?" Gray asked as he followed Patton into the building.

"There is. The library is key to connecting the women."

Patton led Gray to an area in the rear of the building, where he saw Sparks standing next to a cork bulletin board attached to a wall.

"Sterling, you look like one of us now," Sparks said as he eyed Gray's attire. "We were just thinking of calling you when you texted. We've made some headway on the case."

Gray walked up to the board, where there were photographs of the two victims and two missing persons. There was also a map with the library's location highlighted, the residences of all four women, and where the two victims' bodies were discovered.

"I'm eager to hear what you got," Gray said.

Sparks pointed to screengrabs of video footage that had been tacked on the board. "This is Luna leaving Friley Hall at 5:08 p.m. This is her arriving at Parks Library at 6:18 p.m. We're assuming she went to get something to eat during that time frame. Here we have her exiting the library at 10:04 p.m. The library closes at ten, so she stayed until she was kicked out. We checked the footage at Friley Hall all the way to seven in the morning, when her roommate realized she hadn't come back. No sign of Luna ever returning. So that confirms our thinking that she went missing shortly after."

"Any other people exiting the library during that time or hanging around that looked out of place?" Gray asked.

Sparks shook his head. "From Luna's arrival until her departure, a lot of other students came and went."

Patton cleared his throat. "Over here, we were able to place the first victim, Sheila Wang, at the library the night she disappeared. Here she is, leaving at 9:42 p.m. And over here is our second victim, Sofia Garcia, also leaving the library the same night she was thought to have been abducted, 9:50 p.m."

"She's the one that was reported missing by her boyfriend, right?" Gray asked.

"That's correct," Patton answered.

"The only person we haven't been able to pin down to the library is our other missing person, Nia Carter," Sparks said. "We have more footage we're combing through. Plus, Hampton told us she was a regular there. It's only a matter of time. Our guy is operating in a small area. He also isn't heading out of town very far to discard the bodies. We've already requested extra patrols around the library at night and the area where the bodies were found. If he's a creature of habit, which it seems like he is, we might get lucky."

"It's clear this is the hunting ground," Gray said, pointing at the library. "He's camping inside, watching and selecting. Before he makes his move, he knows their routines, whether they come and go with others or alone. I've worked up a rough profile, which will complement what you've already discovered. I've emailed you my work on the guy, but I'll bullet-point it for you right now."

Gray grabbed a dry-erase marker and walked over to a whiteboard:

- *White male between 18 and 25.*
- *Has superiority complex.*
- *Educated but arrogant.*
- *His kills are mission-oriented.*

"Could you expand upon that last point?" Patton asked.

"It essentially means he feels like something is wrong, and it's his job, or purpose, to make it right. It's commonly associated with race or homosexuality, but in this case, I don't think that's what's driving him. Instead, I believe it has to do with school or education in general. Does that make sense?"

Patton nodded, and Gray continued to add to his list.

- *Body mutilation is a statement or an example.*
- *Familiar with Ames; most likely a local.*
- *He's young-looking and blends easily with other students.*

"Do you think he's sending a message by cutting these women up?" Sparks asked.

"It could be twofold." Gray capped the pen and put it down. "He's using that as a way to grab attention and at the same time make a point. I can't be sure exactly what that is yet. But I can tell you that he's angry, either at schools or possibly what they represent. Sadly, these women are caught up in the middle."

"A disgruntled student. Typical. So, where do we go from here?" Sparks asked.

"The security footage will be key. We're looking for a young male who has shown his face in that library numerous times since the university came back in session. This is someone who's there at night but isn't studying. He may be moving around the library as opposed to sitting in one place. He's essentially people-watching. If we can find someone like that, we might have our guy."

"I'll switch gears and start looking for a male," Patton said as he took a seat at his desk and began combing through footage.

Gray glanced at his watch. "It's still early. I think visiting the library tonight is a good idea." He looked over at Sparks. "Do you want to study?"

10

Sparks parked the Crown Victoria along Morrill Drive, which ran parallel with the Parks Library. He and Gray left the car and made their way to the entrance of the library. There was a healthy amount of foot traffic along the pathways crisscrossing the lengthy lawn in front of the building. Students were also coming and going from the library.

"So we're just visitors doing some research," Sparks said as he reached for the door entrance.

"That's the plan."

Inside, the two played it cool while they looked over the first floor. The communal tables in the atrium were packed with students. Bookbags, purses, clothing, laptops, and other personal items littered the tabletops. Students were either in their own world with their earbuds or whispering quietly among their study group.

"Let's split up," Gray said. "I'll check out that side. You take the other end."

Sparks nodded and walked away. Gray made his way down the left side of the library, paying attention to students, primarily the men. He casually looked down the aisles of library stacks. He took his time as he walked, every so often turning entering an aisle and then looping back toward the side. He wished he had brought his laptop as he felt like he stood out walking around empty-handed. But other students were as well. Maybe it was because he knew he wasn't the typical age of a university student.

When Gray reached his end of the library, he took the stairs up to the second floor. He was keen to look at the private study rooms since that was where Luna liked to go. One by one, he walked by, looking through the square glass windows built into each door. They were all filled, some with three students squeezed inside. Just as he was coming to the last of them, a door opened, and the young man exited in a hurry, nearly running smack into Gray.

"Sorry, man. My bad," the kid said.

"No worries" Gray looked him up and down. Jeans and a hoodie, and a backpack slung over one shoulder. "Are you finished in there?"

"Yeah, man, it's all yours."

Gray slipped into the room, closing the door behind him. He took a seat at the small table and took the space in. *So, Luna, this is your home away from home. Did you sit facing the door, or did you sit facing the wall? How does someone watch you when you're cooped up in here?*

Gray stood and placed an ear against the wall. He could hear the student in the next study room talking on the phone. The conversation was muffled, so he couldn't make out what was said, only that the voice was female. But he already knew that, since he had peeked inside when he walked by earlier.

He stood and looked through the view window. There were a few sofas spread out on the other side of the atrium. Could Luna's abductor be sitting there and keeping watch? It was possible. He didn't need to have eyes on her at all times. Knowing her routine was enough.

Gray left the study room, crossed over to the other side of the atrium, and took a seat on a couch. From where he sat, he could see all of the study rooms, ten in total. It was likely her abductor could have been on the couch every night. Some students were sitting on the sofas: one typing on a laptop, another reading a book. Just then, Sparks appeared from an opposite stairwell. He walked over and took a seat next to Gray.

"Any thoughts?" he asked.

"Those are the study rooms where Luna kept herself hidden. Our guy could have been sitting over here every night, noting when she came and left. With a computer open on his lap, she'd pay no attention to him."

"Yeah, you're right. I imagine some nights, these might have been full, forcing her to sit at one of the communal tables. It would be even easier to watch her there. Let's take a look around the third floor."

Sparks and Gray headed up a stairwell. There were some chairs and couches, but mostly rows of library stacks lined with books. They split up and walked the aisles. A few moments later, they reconvened.

"You good to stick around until closing?" Gray asked.

"Not a problem. We're looking for a male student who is watching and not studying."

"I think we should keep it open beyond students. Our guy may not be one," Gray said.

"He may not, but in order to do what he's doing right under everyone's noses, he's gotta be. I'll sit on the second floor; you take the first floor. If you want, we can either trade spots later or stay put."

Gray nodded before heading back to the first floor. He grabbed a book off a shelf and then looked for an open seat at the communal tables. Ten tables spaced out across the atrium; each one had seating for ten people on either side, so twenty students to a table.

Gray made a note of the time and how many male students were in the library. It definitely skewed women, probably seventy percent, and various ethnicities across the board. None of the male students jumped out at Gray. None were watching others like Gray was watching them.

A little over an hour and a half had passed, and the students had changed during that time. But the ratio of women to men remained the same. Gray and Sparks had been communicating with each other through text messages. All was quiet on the second floor. Gray felt antsy, like he was wasting time. Luna was still alive. Perhaps even Carter.

It was nearing ten, and the number of students in the library had shrunk to about twenty. Gray tapped out a message to Sparks asking if anyone was still in the study rooms. He responded, saying two of them were still occupied. One had a guy, the other a girl.

Gray's phone buzzed. It was Sparks calling. "Yeah, what's up?" Gray asked quietly.

"There's a kid I've been watching in one of the study rooms," Sparks said. "He checked them all and chose a room next to a girl."

"So?"

"Well, he just walked out zipping up his pants. He's walking down the stairs right now. Blue hoodie, black backpack, blond hair."

"I see him."

"Snap a picture of him if you can. I missed him."

Gray took a picture of the boy as he passed by.

"Got it."

"I'm looking in the study room right now. I see a lot of crumpled-up tissues in the trash bin. Doesn't take a brain surgeon to figure out what was going on in here."

"None of our victims had any signs of sexual abuse."

"I know, but maybe he gets off on selecting his victims. It's worth keeping an eye on the kid, maybe even having a conversation with him."

"You want me to grab him?"

"We got his photo. Why don't you come on up?"

When Gray arrived at the study rooms, he saw Sparks standing in the doorway to one. He was talking to a young lady inside.

"I appreciate you taking the time to answer questions. This is my colleague Agent Gray. This is Kristina Jensen. Do you want to show her the photo?"

Gray pulled up the photo on his phone and showed it to the woman.

"Oh my God. I know him. He's so weird."

"How exactly do you know him?" Gray asked.

"Well, I don't really know him. I've seen him around the library lately. He's always staring at me. Really creepy vibes. Twice he sat in the study room next to me."

"How did you know?" Sparks asked.

"Because he looks at me through the window in the door, and then I hear him go into room next to me, and, um . . ."

"What is it?" Sparks asked.

"I hear noises that sound like, you know, like he's jacking off."

"Did you know he was just here, in the room next door?"

"Really? I thought I heard moaning. *Gross!* Are you guys here to catch him? He should be expelled from school."

"Have you reported this to anyone?" Gray asked.

"No, not yet."

"Do you know if he's done any of these creepy things to other girls in the library?"

"No. As far as I know it's just me. Has he?"

"We're looking into it," Sparks said. "Do you know if he lives off campus or on campus? Do you have any classes together?"

"No and no. Thank God. It would be so disgusting to have a class with him."

"Hey, I'm going to head back downstairs and keep an eye on him," Gray said.

Gray didn't see the kid right away and figured he'd left already. Since the library was closing shortly, he decided to step outside and watch how the students filed out of the building and which pathway most of them took.

Gray studied the scenery as he stood in front of the entrance. The lawn out front was clear of students. The buildings on either side were dark. There was no reason to walk across the lawn at this hour unless one was leaving the library. Gray drew a deep breath of air and picked up a minty scent from nearby shrubs to his left. Near them was a thicket of oak trees that blocked his view to Morrill Drive. A pathway cut through the trees. To the left was another copse of trees that was sandwiched between two tall buildings. A pathway also led into that grouping. And it was very dark. Gray started to walk out into the field when he heard a woman call out."

"Stop! Get away from me."

Son of a bitch! Gray drew his service weapon and hurried toward the voice coming from the direction of the two tall buildings.

"Stop, I said!" the woman's voice called out again.

Gray was in the middle of the thicket. He couldn't see the woman, but he could definitely hear what sounded like a scuffle ahead. He picked up the pace, raising his weapon.

"Come here!" a man's voice said.

"No!"

Gray was close. They had to be just on the other side of the thicket. He cleared the trees and burst into the open parking lot just as loud laughter rang out.

"I said stop. You know I hate it when you tickle me," the woman said.

A young man had a woman wrapped up in his arms. They were standing under a lamppost. A second later, the two lovers locked lips as Gray came to a stop a few feet from them. He holstered his weapon, the couple still oblivious to his presence. They wobbled in their lovers' lock. A strong indication they had been out drinking. Gray shook his head and went back to the library. As he walked to the entrance, Sparks emerged.

"You see something over there?" Sparks asked

"Nah, just a couple of students messing around. You?"

"I was the last one out. Just a few staff left inside, locking up."

Just then, Sparks's phone rang. "Sparks here. Where? We're on our way." He hung up. "That was Kenny. The body of Nia Carter was just found."

11

Sparks and Gray had raced over to the location that Patton had given them. It wasn't far from where Garcia's body had been found. Blue and red lights lit the green stalks in the field as Sparks brought his car to a stop behind multiple police cruisers parked on the side of the road. Up ahead, Patton could be seen walking toward them.

"Kenny, what do you know?" Sparks asked as he climbed out of his vehicle.

Sparks and Gray walked alongside Patton as they made their way over to the body.

"It definitely looks like Nia Carter," Patton said. "No identification on the body, but I'm pretty sure it's her. Same MO as the other two victims: she was found nude with an incision running from her throat to her pubic bone. Rigor mortis has already started, so I imagine she's been here at minimum of four to five hours. I'm pretty sure when the medical examiner conducts the autopsy, he'll find the same plastic packaging inside. She's right over there."

"He didn't bother to drag the body into the fields this time," Sparks said.

"He's not progressing," Gray said. "Usually, they get better. This could mean he's in a hurry, like he's trying to meet a deadline or something. He's not too worried about getting caught."

"Or he wanted to hurry back to the library before it closed," Sparks said.

"What?" Patton said, noticing Sparks winking at Gray.

"We have person of interest," Sparks said. "A student that likes to get off in the study rooms next to ones occupied by women."

"You think it's him?" Patton asked.

"It sure as hell is looking like it," Sparks said. "We spoke to the girl in the study room next door, and she's seen him stalking her."

"She could be the next victim. What do you think, Sterling?"

"It's possible."

"Who discovered the body?" Sparks asked.

"Carlton James, of all people found her. He's over there in his pickup."

"Who's Carlton?" Gray asked.

"Long-time resident. He's harmless." Sparks said to Gray before turning his attention back to Patton. "Is he drunk?"

"Smashed. That's why I'm surprised he stuck around after calling it in. I already spoke with him. He needed to take a leak and pulled over right where the body happened to be. Started peeing a few feet away. I got a tow truck on the way for his vehicle. He can sleep it off at the station, and we can interview him again in the morning."

Gray moved in closer for a better look at the body. This was his first time seeing a victim up close, and seeing the stitching running the length of her torso hit harder. Photographs had a way of taking away the impact of death.

"What are you thinking?" Sparks asked as he came up behind Gray.

"He may be spooked, but I don't get the impression it's because he thinks you guys are on to him."

"What is it?"

"I'm not entirely sure. There's something else at play here. Something I haven't quite cracked."

"Unless we catch him, I think we got another day or so before we're looking at Luna's body," Sparks said. "We need to talk to study-room boy real quick."

"You're right about that," Gray said. "But that also means he's hunting for another victim. It's clear from the timeline we've established that he's keeping two girls with him at once. If we can prevent him from grabbing another girl, we might be able to buy Luna more time."

"Well, Ms. Jensen confirmed that boy has been keeping tabs on her. While we locate him, I'll place a security detail on Jensen," Sparks said.

"Those are good precautionary tactics, but I'm not ready to put all our bets on this kid we found tonight. We need to still keep the net cast wide."

"No problem. I'll increase our police presence on the campus and at the library, maybe even have uniformed officers camped inside. I'll talk to Hampton and see if she can initiate a procedure where people have to check in with identification when they enter the library. These will all act as deterrents."

"Anything we can do to slow our killer down and buy us time is helpful."

Gray woke early the following morning. He'd had a restless night, waking every hour on the hour until he finally gave up and rolled out of bed at five. With a pot of black coffee ordered from room service, he checked his email, answering one from his supervisor. There was another email from a woman he was dating back in Quantico. She wanted to end things between them. He deleted it.

Gray refilled his mug before looking over his notes on the investigation. He wanted to focus on a statement he'd made to Sparks earlier at the Carter crime scene: the killer was keeping two victims with him at the same time. What exactly was his reasoning for doing so? If both abductees were alive at some time, did the most recent abductee always witness the murder of the other person? Did Luna witness the death of Carter?

Does forcing Luna to watch him kill Carter give him pleasure? He must be receiving some sort of gratification from it. He has a captive audience. Luna has no choice but to watch. The way he kills his victims is much like he's conducting a crude autopsy. Is that what he's doing? Was Carter already dead before Luna was taken? Did she only witness the autopsy? This is an interesting angle. Let's stay with it. Our killer always has two victims with him. Both may be alive at some point, but also, at some point, only one may be alive. If Luna's role was as a witness, then Carter's role was to . . . to—that's it! Carter was there to showcase, to demonstrate. Luna was there to observe or learn. ISU students. Studying in the library. Studious. How could I have not seen this earlier?

Gray glanced over at his bedside clock: six a.m. He grabbed his phone and dialed Sparks.

"Sparks speaking."

"Simon, it's Sterling. Sorry to call so early."

"No worries, I'm an early riser. What's up?"

"I think I figured out what's motivating our guy. He's conducting a class. He's teaching human biology."

12

Sparks and Patton showed up at Gray's hotel about forty-five minutes later, giving him plenty of time to shower and get dressed. Gray was waiting in the lobby with a cup of coffee when the two detectives entered.

"Simon. Kenny. I appreciate you coming over so quickly. They have a coffee bar over there. Can I interest you guys?"

A little later, the three of them settled into some chairs with coffees in hand.

"I'm really interested to hear this teacher theory you have cooking in your head," Sparks said after taking a sip.

"Look, we know he's keeping two women with him at the same time. I do think it's possible that, for a short period, they're both alive. But I don't think that's really his intention."

Gray quickly explained his reasoning for why the victims were being cut open and then sewn back up.

"Wait a minute," Sparks said, holding up a hand. "You really think he's teaching a class on human biology, and Luna is the student, and Carter was . . . the frog?"

"I do. That's why he always has two victims with him. Carter was the student at one point, and Garcia, the victim, dragged into the cornfield, was the . . . we'll call it the assignment. That means the first victim, Wang, was the assignment for Garcia. I'm assuming Wang was the guinea pig. He needed her to start his class."

"He won't kill Luna until he has someone else to teach," Sparks said.

"That's right. Anything we can do to disrupt and prevent him from abducting another student will help."

"But he can take a student from anywhere. There are about thirty thousand to choose from," Patton said.

"Not unless he's locked on to Jensen," Sparks said.

"He's looking for students he feels are excelling in school, and he's making that selection by keeping watch in the library."

"Which is where Jensen was at."

"Wow, this is really starting to look like this study-room kid is our guy," Patton said.

"How soon can you guys find out who he is and where he's at?"

"As soon as the administrative offices are open, I'm on it," Patton said.

Sparks shook his head. "I'm sorry, but I'm just having a hard time wrapping my brain around the classroom theory. I know this is your thing, but I can't help but feel you might be overthinking this."

"It's out there. I get it. But I have to also assume that this student you have in your sights isn't our guy. A much as you feel all signs are pointing to him, he doesn't quite fit the profile."

"Well, we'll run down the lead anyway."

"Absolutely, but we should also carry on as if we don't have this guy identified yet and as if he may not be a student."

"All right," Sparks said. "Continue with your analysis."

"Our guy appears to be disillusioned with either ISU or education in general. He might have had trouble learning while growing up. Either he felt he wasn't getting a proper education, or he felt his teachers were disingenuous in their efforts. Another reason could be that he applied for a job at ISU he believed he was qualified for and was rejected. Or he wanted to attend ISU and was rejected. Either of those three could easily be what spurred him to take matters into his own hands. The writing on the plastic bag, lesson one, and so forth. Those weren't lessons for law enforcement. Those were basic lessons he had given. When the autopsy is conducted on Carter. I'm positive 'lesson three' will have been written on the bag."

Sparks's face tightened. "So he's showing, or trying to show, through his own sick way how teaching should be done?"

"Correct. He believes he's righting a wrong. This is completely in line with him being a mission-oriented killer. He feels he needs to fix a broken system."

"Man, you gotta be some kind of messed up to get your head in a space like that," Patton said as he ran his hand through his hair.

"He's delusional, no doubt about that," Gray said.

"So now what?" Sparks said. "We know we can run interference and disrupt his lesson plan. But how long can we keep that up? How long before he decides to cancel his class and just get rid of Luna and move on?"

"I don't know, but I still think we have an advantage. We know he's hunting in the library. He's had Luna for a while now. He'll need to prepare Luna for his next student, but he won't do that until he has a new student in his possession. I highly doubt he has the facilities to keep a dead body around without it starting to decay. As soon as he grabs someone new, he'll kill Luna and prepare her for the next lesson plan."

"If we branch out from students, then we should start looking at teaching applications at the university in the last year," Patton said. There might be a situation where an interview went bad and threats were made, or there was an unusual amount of stomping out of the office."

"Honestly, the more I think about it, the more I think this guy isn't qualified to teach, not even as a teacher's assistant. Our guy is young. My advice is to dig into job applications that center around jobs in maintenance, the on-campus restaurants, or even a standard administrative job."

"I'll get right on it right after I identify the kid in the photo."

"We already have uniformed officers scheduled into the library today. A security detail has been assigned to Jensen. She's been instructed to take time off from her classes for a couple of days and remain in her dorm room," Sparks said. "I still need to follow up with Hampton on identifying people as they come into the library."

"I'll tag along with you, Simon, if you don't mind," Gray said. "I'd like to spend extra time at the library. It might trigger something else that can help."

After dropping Patton off at the station, Sparks and Gray made their way to the library. It was still early, and they had about thirty minutes before it opened.

"You know what I don't get," Sparks said as he brought the car to a stop and engaged the parking brake. "How long did this guy think he could carry on doing what he's doing? You know, half-assing it? Had he dragged Carter's body into the fields, who knows when she would have been found?"

"He's focused on his task. His failure to dispose of the body in a better way is proof of that. I'm confident we'll catch him. The question is, will that be done in time to save Luna?"

___

13

To Bowen's surprise, he woke that morning with an extra bounce in his step and a positive outlook on what he was doing. Last night he had made his selection of the two candidates, and all he had to do was pick her up. But what really had him jazzed that morning were Luna's words to him the day before: *I got a lot out of it. I learned.*

I knew it wasn't my shortcomings or my poor grades. The teacher could not teach. I just proved my case with my student.

Bowen finished scrambling the eggs in the bowl and then poured them into the frying pan. He was preparing breakfast for Luna, which was new for him. He never fed the other students. A couple of bottles of water at best was all they received. But she was different and therefore deserved different treatment.

A little later, Bowen carried a serving tray with a plate of scrambled eggs and crispy bacon, two slices of toast with butter and strawberry jam, and a small bowl of sliced fruit. He even went the distance and made fresh-squeezed orange juice.

"Good morning," Bowen said as he entered the room with a smile on his face. He used his shoulder to flip on the lights. "I'm sorry about my delay in getting back to you. I was occupied. But I've made it up to you: breakfast! What do you say, Student? Are you hungry?"

"Yes," Luna answered. "I thought you had forgotten all about me."

Bowen placed the tray on the floor before fishing the key out of his pants pocket. He slipped the key into the padlock and turned it until it popped open. Then, he picked the tray back up without opening the cage door.

"Please give me a hand and push the door open."

Luna did as she was told and took the tray from him. She placed it on the desk chair and immediately started eating. Bowen closed the cage door and locked it before bringing a chair over to the cage so he could sit.

"Tell me, Student, are you enjoying your food? Breakfast is the most important meal of the day."

"Yes, Mr. Bowen. It's delicious. Did you cook this yourself?"

He smiled. "I've been known to dabble in the kitchen."

"Will we have another lesson today?" she asked in between bites.

"That is an excellent question. I have given it thought, and sadly, I haven't quite made up my mind."

"I understand. I'm sure there are a lot of things to consider when planning your next lesson."

"Absolutely. You really do get it, don't you?"

"Of course. I've noticed that teachers nowadays don't put that much thought into how they conduct their lessons. They follow a generic syllabus rather than taking the time to create one that's actually catered to their current students. But you do."

"Wow. Just wow. I couldn't agree more. I've always thought that, even as a young boy. Unfortunately, too few people truly understand that."

"It always starts with one person doing the right thing. From there, it becomes two, and two becomes three, and so on. But one person needs to make the leap. I believe that's exactly what you're doing, Mr. Bowen. You've leaped."

"I have, haven't I? I must say I'm enjoying our morning chat."

"So am I. I hope we have many more."

Bowen smiled as he wagged a finger at Luna. "Are you guilty of trying to become a teacher's pet?"

"It's hard not to when the teacher is so likable."

Bowen stood. "Well, I have things to do, and you need to finish your breakfast. I will continue thinking about your proposal. There are adjustments to my lesson plan that must be made if I am to continue teaching you. But I will tell you this . . ." He smiled and whispered, "It's leaning toward your favor."

Luna kept her eye on Bowen until he disappeared behind the closed door. She knew she missed an opportunity to run to the gurney when he showed up. But Luna had decided to bide her time. She felt buttering him up more would increase her chances of escape. She couldn't risk anything going wrong. Even escaping from the room was no guarantee she'd be safe. She had no idea where she was. She could be in the middle of a cornfield. She had to take Bowen out, or at the very least, incapacitate him if she wanted a chance at survival. The last thing she wanted was to run outside and find out she was in the middle of nowhere, only to realize Bowen was then hunting her with a rifle.

He had bought into her story about his excellent teaching methods. All she had to do was continue to push those buttons. But Luna was no dummy. She knew if she failed to extend her teaching lessons or escape beforehand, she'd be the next body on that gurney for another student. She had figured out his sicko ways. He wasn't considering her proposal. He was still trying to get another girl back to his place. As soon as he did that, she was as good as dead.

Just thinking about that made Luna's cheeks burn. It didn't frighten her. What it did was anger her. She wanted nothing more than to kick Mr. Bowen in the crotch and then stomp on his face. He deserved no less for what he'd done to all those innocent girls. And to blame it on the fact that he had done poorly in school as a little boy. That was his fault, not the fault of the education system. To blame others for his shortcomings and inability to succeed was a pathetic excuse.

The next time you open that cage door will be the last. I swear to it, Mr. Bowen. Do you think I'm gunning to be the teacher's pet? No, you have it all wrong. I'm the teacher's worst nightmare: a student that doesn't give a shit.

14

By ten a.m. that morning, an Ames police cruiser had been parked near the Parks Library as a deterrent. If that wasn't enough, two uniformed officers were stationed inside the library. In addition to that, Hampton agreed to establish new procedures for the next few days. Anyone entering the library needed to show their identification and enter their name in a registry. Plus, a portable security camera had been set up at the front counter near the entrance. Anyone coming in and out would be picked up on camera.

Gray and Sparks were sitting at one of the communal tables in the library's atrium.

"It feels like we're a couple of spiders hoping our prey walks into our web," Sparks said.

"Yeah, it does a little. If he makes a move, it might be at night."

Sparks's phone buzzed. "It's Kenny," he said before answering. "Did you find him? Okay, we'll meet you there."

"Kenny ID'd our pervert. His name is Elijah Howard. He lives in an apartment off campus. Let's go."

Sparks and Gray made the short drive to an apartment complex about a half mile from the campus. It was two-story brick building shaped like an L. Patton was already there.

"I was able to secure a no-knock warrant, if you prefer that route," he said

"I do," Sparks answered.

"The apartment manager is waiting for us inside."

Once inside the building, they were greeted by a heavyset man holding a large ring of keys.

"I'm Alvin Ward. I manage the building."

"How well do you know Mr. Howard?"

"Same as I would the forty other tenants. Pays his rent on time and gives me no trouble. That's all I care about."

Ward led them up the stairs to the second floor to a corner unit.

"As soon as you unlock the door. I want you to step off to the side. Do not under any circumstances enter that apartment. Understood?" Sparks said to Ward.

Sparks knocked on the door. "Elijah Howard. This is Detective Simon Sparks with the Ames Police Department. We need to speak with you."

Sparks removed his service weapon and then motioned for Ward to unlock the door. As soon as he did that, Sparks pushed the door open and entered. Patton and Gray followed.

Sparks made a beeline through the empty living room straight to the bedroom. The door was open. Sitting at a desk, with his back to the doorway, was Howard. He had headphones on and was on his laptop, looking at porn. But that's not what had Sparks caught with his mouth hanging open. Taped to the wall in front of him were at least fifteen printouts of photographs taken of Kristina Jensen. In addition, there were printouts of articles on the case Sparks and Patton had been investigating. There were also printed photos of the other victims.

Two and a half hours passed since Howard had been taken into custody and brought to the police station. He had spent most of that time sitting in an interrogation room, being questioned by Sparks. Gray and Patton were standing in the observation room, watching.

"Elijah, come on. I know you're tired of keeping these secrets and hiding what you've done. We're here to help you. Coming clean will take this terrible weight off your shoulders. You'll feel better. I promise."

"I know you think I killed those women because of the stuff on my wall, but I didn't. I promise. I only followed the case because it was interesting."

"Elijah, you like Kristina, right? Is that a safe assumption?"

"Yeah."

"I get it. She's an attractive woman. Man, when I was your age, I was awkward around women. I didn't always know what to say and when I did get the courage to speak to them, I always said something dumb. You're not alone. Trust me. When you sat in the study room next to here, I bet you were trying to figure out how to ask her out, or maybe even have a simple conversation, right?"

"Yeah."

"But you were worried you'd say something corny or clam up and choke on your words. That sounds a lot like me when I was your age. When you talked to those other women—Nia Carter, Sofia Garcia, Sheila Wang—did you have the same problem?"

"I never talked to them."

"You knew them, though. You've seen them around campus, right?"

"Sure, but I see a lot of people around campus."

"According to school, you had a class with Sofia Garcia and Nia Carter."

"I have classes with a lot of people. It's a school."

"Why did you keep photos of Kristina Jensen on your wall?"

"Is it a crime to take photo of someone? She was in a public space. And the other photos were from articles in the school's newspaper. I didn't take them."

"It must have been frustrating to want to know these women and not be able to. Is that what this is about? Did you take out your frustrations on them? And maybe it made you feel a little bit better."

"I'm telling you I didn't hurt those other women."

"What do you mean when you say you didn't hurt them? Do you mean they didn't feel any pain when you ended their lives?"

"No! You're twisting my words around. I didn't even know them. I had nothing to do with their murders."

"Hey, calm down, now. I don't mean to get you upset. Do you want another bottle of water?"

Howard nodded.

"I'll be right back. Sit tight."

Sparks took the empty bottle with him when he left. He then came into the observation room.

"What do you think?"

"He may not have taken those photos of the other girls, but he definitely took the ones of Jensen," Patton said. "He might have only thought to take photos when he started to target her. Regardless, it's still weird to have photos of the victims. It's like he built his own little shrine."

"Gray? What are your thoughts?"

"I can't deny that he doesn't have a great excuse for the photos, but we need more evidence than just photos. We need something stronger to tie him to the girls, but . . ."

"But what?"

"In my professional opinion, I don't think this is our guy. He may be a pervert, and maybe he was targeting Jensen for something more deviant—"

"What? Like rape?" Patton said.

"I wouldn't take that off the table, but I was thinking along the lines of exposing himself to her either physically or electronically with photos of himself. But I don't believe he's our killer."

"How can you be so sure?"

"I haven't seen him exhibit any of the characteristics I outlined in my profile."

"Not to question your abilities," Sparks said, "but is there a chance that he might not be a perfect match with your profile and still be the killer?"

"Yes. I'm not saying to cut him loose. Do what you need to do. Continue questioning and digging into his background. There's certainly more to learn about him. Cross-check his DNA with DNA from the crime scenes."

Just then Patton received a call on his phone

"Detective Patton speaking. Uh-huh. Really? Now, that's interesting. And this was more than one occurrence? I see. Hey, appreciate your help with this. Okay. Message me the name of his supervisor, and we'll follow up over here."

"Something come up?" Gray asked as Patton got off the call.

"I had an officer helping me with the job application lead. He started looking at firings from the school over the last year. A young man employed in the custodial engineering department was let go earlier this year for entering classrooms and leaving messages on the whiteboard. He had to be physically removed. A disgruntled employee fits your profile."

"It does. You got a name for him?"

"Gary Bowen. The officer already ran a background check on him. He's clean. No prior arrests."

"This may or may not be something, but it's worth us having a chat with his supervisor," Gray said. "I'll run this lead down while you two stick with Howard."

Custodial services was located in the Office of Sustainability, about a ten-minute walk from the library. Gray borrowed Sparks's vehicle and arrived at a one-story building outfitted with delivery docks and several trucks parked outside belonging to outside contractors. The person Gray needed to meet with was Diane Moss, a senior manager in custodial services.

After a quick introduction at reception, Gray took a seat and waited. A few seconds later, a short brunette in a gray pantsuit appeared.

"Ms. Moss," Sparks said as he stood.

"Yes, that's me. How can I be of help?"

"I'm Special Agent Gray. I need to ask you a few questions about a previous employee."

"No problem. Come on back to my office."

Gray took a seat as Moss closed the door.

"Who are we talking about?" she asked as she sat behind her desk.

"Gary Bowen. Do you remember him?"

"I sure do. He worked for me for about a year before we had to let him go. It wasn't pleasant. He, as anyone would be about losing their job, was upset."

"I understand," Gray said. "Could you tell me why you let Mr. Bowen go?"

"While cleaning classrooms, he had started to leave messages on the whiteboards. I'm not talking about having-a-nice-day sort of stuff. They were rants. It made him appear very angry, which was strange because at first he was a pretty quiet guy."

"What exactly was Mr. Bowen ranting about?"

"It came across very manifesto-like. He wrote stuff about how the system was rigged and that nothing appears to be what it is. From the few I was able to see, it was vague, but you could tell he was trying to make some sort of point. It's hard to explain. To me, it was just a bunch of gibberish. I gave him a warning and told him to stop."

"He carried on?"

"Yup. And it got worse. Sometimes a professor would leave a lesson on the board. He would add to it, change it around, and put his own spin on it. It was like his version of *Good Will Hunting*, only it wasn't clever. Do you know what I mean? I had no choice as it was disrupting the classes. I had to let him go."

"Other than his professional character, what can you tell me about Mr. Bowen?"

"He was quiet and kept to himself. He was polite. Always answered questions but never tried to carry on a conversation, let alone start one. That didn't bother me. People have a different way of interacting with colleagues. He came off as a very private person. To be honest, I manage hundreds of people, so it's a little hard to get to know all of them."

"Going back to the rants," Gray said. "Did any of them talk about education either here at ISU or in general?"

Moss took a moment to consider the question. "I want to say that subject sounds familiar, but I can't be sure. It was a long time ago, and I didn't document what he was writing. Most of the time, I never saw it. The professor or the teacher's assistant would erase it before filing a report."

"Did Mr. Bowen look young?"

"You mean did he have a baby face? No, he didn't, but if you're asking, could he pass for a student? Yeah, I don't think he was older than twenty-five. I don't have files on him. If you reach out to the university's human resources department, they'd be able to provide that sort of information. Do you think Mr. Bowen is connected to the disappearing students?"

"I can't comment on an active investigation," Gray said.

"Of course. Unless there's anything else you'd like to ask me, I do have a staff meeting I need to prepare for."

Gray smiled as he stood. "You've been helpful, Ms. Moss. We appreciate your time."

Once outside of the building Gray checked his phone for messages, specifically for whether an address for Bowen had been found, but he had none. *It might be faster if I just head over to human resources myself.*

15

Bowen was at home, sitting in his leather recliner playing the same game on his phone. He operated his phone with one hand while the other held a grilled cheese sandwich—his second of the day.

It was a little after three p.m. Night couldn't come fast enough. He was close to making a decision on the request Luna had made. He was ninety percent sure he would grant it.

There were a couple hiccups. He had never brought a new student back to his class without getting rid of the previous one. Logistics needed to be worked out.

It would be strange for me to prepare the body for class in front of her. Maybe I'll slip her a sleeping pill. I can prepare the body quickly. She won't even know until the morning when I surprise her with class.

Then there was the lesson itself.

I can't make her sit through the exact same class. She wouldn't learn. She's already told me I'm the best she's ever had. I definitely don't want to let her down.

Bowen had been wrangling with that ever since he fired up the mobile game on his phone.

What if I take teaching one step further and literally make it a teaching lesson? Have her participate in the dissection. Surely that would be of interest to her—a hands-on approach to human biology. Sounds like an incredible opportu-

nity to me. Could she handle it, though? Does she have the stomach to power through something like that? Well, she's eager, so that says a lot. Yes, I think that's what I'll do. She'll assist me.

The doorbell snapped Bowen out of the mental pats on his back. Standing outside on his doorstep was a man he'd never seen before.

"Yes, can I help you?" Bowen asked as he peeked through the cracked door.

"Are you Mr. Gary Bowen?"

"I am. Who are you?"

"I'm Special Agent Gray. You're not in any trouble. I just want to ask you a few questions. In fact, we're talking to everyone in the neighborhood. May I come inside?"

"Uh, my place is kind of a mess. I'd be much more comfortable if we had the conversation right here." Bowen was still holding his grilled cheese sandwich and took a quick bite.

"You live alone?"

"Uh, yeah, why?"

"Just inquiring. I'm here to talk to you about your previous employer, ISU. It's my understanding that you were employed by the university in their custodial services department, correct?"

"Yes, that's right. Are you investigating why I was fired? Because if you are, I was under the impression we had parted amicably."

"No, no, you got it all wrong. No one's investigating why you were let go. I just need a little background information."

"Well, I'm sure you already spoke to my old supervisor, Ms. Moss."

"We did, but it's always good to hear both sides of the story."

"Did she mention I was named Employee of the Month after three months on the job? No? Typical. Why is it that people only remember the bad and never the good?"

"What would be bad? Could you expand on that?"

Bowen let out a loud breath. "Apparently, writing on the whiteboard in a classroom is a big no-no. You'd think that would be the one place to express your thoughts: a classroom. Apparently, I was wrong. That's why they fired me."

"I see. Were you able to find employment elsewhere?"

"I'm still looking while I collect unemployment. After that, I might have to start considering working in Des Moines. That's not a daily commute I'm looking forward to."

"Did you know any of the students?" Gray asked. "Make some friends."

"I knew some, but it was mostly saying hi in the halls. We weren't supposed to fraternize with the students."

"ISU is a big campus. Did you work in the same building all the time?" Gray continued with his questions.

"Not always. We rotated to different buildings. I was pleased when I got assigned to the Parks Library."

"And why was that?"

"I like to read, so I always snuck time to browse the books. I think that's why they moved me to another building. Someone probably complained. I should have been there for six weeks. Instead, I was rotated out shortly after three weeks."

"The general public is free to visit the library, so you could always go back during your spare time."

"Yeah, and I did, but, you know, being there while at work . . . It was a nice way to break up the day."

"Have you visited recently?"

"No, it's been a while. I've been busy with my job search." Bowen popped the last of his sandwich in his mouth. "Anything else?" he asked with his mouth full.

"One last question. Is that your vehicle parked in the driveway?"

16

As Gray walked away from Bowen's home, he took note of the area. The quirky man lived on a quiet road near the edge of town and within walking distance into a cornfield. Not the one where the bodies were dumped, though. The homes in this area sat on at least an acre of land, affording residents a lot of privacy. Large oak trees were abundant on his property, which would come in handy if one were lugging a body into the house. Gray called Sparks to give him an update on his visit to Bowen's home.

"Young, unemployed man living alone in what is probably a two- or three-bedroom home seems a bit odd," Gray said.

"It does," Sparks said. "We can check the records at town hall and see if Bowen is the actual owner of the property. What was your gut telling you? You think Bowen is our guy?"

"He's a little strange, but that's not enough to pin the bodies on him. He also didn't fight the reason for his firing, nor did he dismiss what he did as trivial. He owned up to it. I expected the opposite."

"If Bowen's our guy, you think he's on to us?" Sparks asked.

"It's possible, but there is one thing that's working in our favor: Luna hasn't shown up anywhere, so he's still working on his mission. I have a thought. Assuming Bowen hasn't been to the library today, he won't know about the uniformed officers. We don't want to spook him if Bowen is our guy, but our presence here might be enough to light a fire under his butt. We can focus our efforts on him for the next twenty-four hours. If we're right about the timeline, then that's about all the time Luna has left."

Gray glanced back over his shoulder while on the phone and spotted Bowen peeking out from a window. "He's watching me right now. I'm going to go talk to a few neighbors just to throw him off. I'll need to leave, but if you send Kenny over, he can keep watch on Bowen without him knowing."

Gray visited two nearby neighbors before returning to his car. Bowen was still watching him.

His phone rang as he settled into the driver's seat. It was Patton. He was at the end of the road.

"Wait until you see me pass by before you slide in over here," Gray said. "It's a light blue house with white trim. Can't miss it. There's a silver Ford Taurus in the driveway."

"Got it," Patton said. "Oh, Bowen's car came back clean. Not even a single parking ticket."

"Either he's smarter than he appears to be or he's one cautious guy," Gray said. "If Bowen leaves his home, tail him."

Bowen kept watch on his visitor as he visited his neighbors and then drove off. He thought it was a unique visit. *Why would the FBI want to question me about my previous employment? Was he doing the same with my neighbors? Wait, calm down. You're overreacting. If he suspected you were responsible for the murders, the FBI would have kicked the door in with their guns drawn. He's fishing. That's all that's happening. Don't let this distract you, Gary. You're doing the right thing. Soon it'll be sundown. Everything is still on track for tonight.*

Gray had been at the library since the late afternoon. Every so often he would check in with Patton and hear the same answer: Bowen hadn't left his house.

"It's seven," Gray said. "If he comes here, it might not be until later. We know he strikes after the library closes. I think I'll join you at Bowen's residence. I'll drop off Simon's car and then take a taxi. It's dark out, and I didn't notice any streetlamps directly outside Bowen's home. It'll be an easy approach by foot."

"Knock yourself out."

"See you in a bit."

17

The taxi came to a stop about a five-minute walk away from the Bowen residence. Gray had already sent a text message letting Patton know he was on the way. A few minutes later, Gray put eyes on Patton's vehicle. He looked over at Bowen's home across the street and spotted the Taurus still parked in the driveway. The house was dark, except for a lamp illuminating one of the windows. Gray kept his eyes on the place until he reached Patton's car and then slipped into the front passenger seat.

Gray had brought two black coffees with him. "Thought you could use a pick-me-up."

"Thanks," Patton said, taking the paper cup from Gray.

"Anything exciting taken place?" Gray asked, motioning toward the home with his head.

Patton squinted as he took a sip of the hot black liquid. "Every now and then, I catch a glimpse of him through the windows, but other than that, it's quiet."

"Any news from Simon?"

"He's still questioning Howard, but I haven't heard anything more that would continue steering the boat in that direction. Do you really think this is our guy?"

"The more I think about it, the more convinced I'm becoming. Admitting to the firing, even taking blame demonstrates signs of narcissism. He believes he's untouchable and in control."

"Sheesh, if he is our guy, Luna could be locked away inside that house. Part of me wants to kick that door down and search the damn place."

"I know the feeling," Gray said as he took a sip from his cup.

"I wish we had something that remotely tied into the investigation. We might have been able to secure a warrant."

"He'll make a move. His ego will force him too."

Ever since Luna heard the noises upstairs, she began to mentally prepare herself for what was to come. Bowen had returned home. Luna had already convinced herself of two possible outcomes. He had another girl who would take her place or become her lesson. Either way, push had come to shove. Luna had to act.

She'd been replaying the scene over and over in her head. Punch his face or scratch at his eyes. She'd know when the moment arrived. After, she'd kick him in the crotch or stomach. Again, she'd know when the moment arrived. Luna sat in the desk chair, eyes on the door. She remained calm, focused, and one hundred percent committed. There could be no hesitation. And if the opportunity to kill Bowen presented itself, Luna would make him pay.

A creak in the floorboard pierced right through the door. Slowly, Bowen made his way down the steps.

Thump.

Thump.

Thump.

Luna balled both fists tightly before relaxing them.

Thump.

Thump.

Thump.

Were his steps heavier? Was he carrying someone?

Thump.

Thump.

Thump.

One thing was clear. She could only hear one set of footsteps. Bowen stopped on the other side door. What was he waiting for?

She heard the scuff of a shoe. The doorknob jiggled before turning, and then the door swung open slowly. There standing in the doorway was Bowen. He was carrying something, but it wasn't a student. And he was smiling.

"Student, I hope you're hungry, because you'll need to keep your energy up," he said. "I have fried country ham and scrambled eggs for you. I even squeezed oranges for juice."

Luna cocked her head. "What's happening?"

"I've made a decision. I will be giving you another class tomorrow morning."

Luna studied Bowen. He had no weapons on him, and he appeared distracted. *He doesn't suspect a thing.*

Bowen placed the tray onto the floor before fishing a key out of his pocket. She got up and moved over to the cage door.

"Do I need to know anything to prepare for class?" she asked as she watched him place the key into the padlock.

"Just be alert and have an open mind."

Bowen turned the key, and the padlock popped open. He slipped the shackle out of the hasp and placed the padlock on the floor before opening the latch. The pressure released from the door hinge cracked the cage door an inch. Luna watched Bowen bend down to pick up the tray, moving his eyes off her in the process.

Now!

Luna kicked the door open, sending it smack into the top of Bowen's head. He yelped as he fell backward onto his butt. Bowen's head hit the floor with a *thunk*. Luna got a quick glimpse of his eyes rolling back into his head. She wasn't expecting that to happen.

Without hesitation, Luna charged at Bowen. She raised her foot up and slammed her heel down on his face. But Bowen was somehow able to deflect her stomp at the last minute. He'd hooked an arm around her calf and yanked, causing Luna to lose her footing and fall to the side, away from the gurney, where the scalpel was.

Change of plans. Get up! Get out! She told herself and she clawed her way toward the door. But Bowen's hand clamped down around her ankle and pulled her leg out from under her. Her chest hit the floor hard, knocking the air out of her lungs. But Luna wasn't deterred. Her eyes were locked on the doorway. She had to get out if she wanted to live.

Bowen had managed to grab hold of both of Luna's legs but she fought, kicking like her life depended on it. It did. She struck him twice in the face, causing him to lose his grip on her. A second later, Luna was back on all fours. She glanced over her shoulder.

Bowen had one hand covering his face, trying to stop the flow of blood leaking everywhere.

"You bitch!" he cried out.

Luna crawled on her hands and knees toward the doorway. As she was about to stand up, Bowen latched onto her ankle once more.

"You're dead!" he shouted.

"Is helping local law enforcement a big part of your job?" Patton asked.

"It's becoming increasingly more common for agents in my department to help with ongoing investigations. I enjoy it."

"What do you like most about it?"

Before Gray could answer, his attention was drawn away by a high-pitched scream.

The front door of the Bowen home opened, and a young woman ran out, screaming at the top of her lungs.

"Holy shit!" Patton shouted. "That's Sara Luna!"

A second later, Bowen appeared. He paused briefly, and Gray swore he looked directly at him before chasing after Luna.

"Help!" Luna cried out once more as she disappeared around the right side of the house.

Gray was out of the vehicle first. He ran toward the right side of the house where Bowen and Luna had disappeared.

"I'll head around the left side," Patton shouted as he cut to the left.

The right side of the house had two large oak trees blocking out any ambient lighting from the streetlights or the moon. Gray drew his weapon and proceeded cautiously into the dark. He had already lost sight of the two. When he reached the rear of the house, his greatest fear for Luna materialized. She'd run into the cornfield.

Gray picked up the pace and ran into the cornfield, making his way down a row of corn stalks. The ground was uneven, and his footing wasn't steady. The tall stalks and the minimal moonlight limited his sight to just a few feet ahead of him.

A cry for help came from the right of Gray. He slowed and pushed through two stalks into the next row, batting leaves and large ears out of his face. Again Luna screamed. Gray continued to cut across the rows, running nearly blind as he moved toward the cries.

Gray came to a stop in a row. His breaths were heavy as he looked back and forth in both directions. He needed to hear Luna again to gauge his distance from her. He was about to push through into the next row when Luna yelled out again.

She's just up ahead.

Gray bolted down the row of stalks, his weapon out front. Luna screamed once more. He was close. A second later, she yelled again. It sounded like she was running toward him but in a different row.

Gray could now hear the trampling of feet on the ground and the rustling of the stalks. They grew louder with every step he took forward until he cut sharply to the right through the stalks, nearly losing his footing as he stumbled into the next row over.

Luna slammed right into him and screamed as she fought to get away from Gray.

"Sara, I'm Agent Gray. It's okay. I'm here to help. Sara!" Gray shouted as he tried to calm her down and prevent her from running off.

It took a moment or so for her mind to make the connection. "Oh my God. Thank you," she said with tears streaming down her face.

"Where's Gary Bowen?"

"I don't know! I don't know!"

Gray put his arm around Sara. "Come on. Let's move."

"He's crazy, you know," she said through heavy breaths.

"Everything's going to be okay."

No sooner had those words left Gray's mouth than the sound of stomping footsteps could be heard right behind them. Gray looked over his shoulder just in time to catch of glimpse of Bowen before he tucked his shoulder and plowed into them. The force of the impact sent Gray and Luna to the ground, tumbling end over end and causing Gray to lose his grip on his weapon.

Stunned but conscious, Gray managed to get to his feet quickly, spinning around toward Bowen. He stood hunched, only a few feet away. His face was covered in blood as he drew mouthfuls of air. In his right hand, he held a cleaver that glinted under the moonlight. Gray hadn't seen that when Bowen exited his home.

"Gary. Don't do it," Gray said. "It'll only make the situation worse." Gray moved into a defensive position. "Be smart about this. No one needs to get hurt. There's been too much of that already."

Bowen kept quiet, his eyes locked onto Gray.

"Put the cleaver down, Gary," he said calmly.

"You ruined everything," Bowen said through gritted teeth. He raised the cleaver above his head as he shot forward. Gray backed up from the charge as he brought both hands up.

Bam!

In a blink of an eye, Bowen had dropped to the ground like a puppet with its strings cut. Gray looked behind him, where the gunshot had come from. Standing with his legs apart and his weapon out in front was Patton.

"You guys okay?" he asked. His gun was still trained on a motionless Bowen.

Gray placed a hand on Patton's shaking hands and lowered the gun. "We're okay. It's over."

Luna was lying on the ground, unconscious. Gray bent down to check on her while Patton called the shooting in on his phone.

"Sara?" Gray lifted her head.

Her eyes opened, and she jerked out of fear.

"Hey, calm down," Gray said. "You're safe."

18

Despite being abducted and held for nearly three days, Sara Luna escaped with only bruising and a case of dehydration. However, the trauma from that event would stay with her for a while, perhaps the rest of her life. Gray was sitting at her bedside in the hospital when she woke the following morning.

"Hi," he said with a smile.

Luna blinked as her eyes focused. "Agent Gray?"

"Hey, you remembered. How are you feeling?"

"Besides relief? I'm fine, I guess."

"The doctors looked you over, physically you're okay, and they'll release you today. Your family has already been notified, and it's my understanding they're on their way. Probably be here any minute."

Just then, Sparks and Patton entered the room.

"Good morning, Sara. I'm Detective Sparks, and this is Detective Patton."

"Hello," Luna said.

"We're all happy to see that you're okay. I realize the last thing you want to do is talk about what happened, but if you could answer a few questions for us, we would appreciate it."

Luna nodded. She proceeded to tell them how Bowen had taken her from the side of the road while walking back to Friley Hall late at night. She told them how he thought he was a professor teaching human biology in a real classroom.

"Yeah, we found that room you're talking about," Sparks said. "And you're saying he believed you were one of his students?"

"Yeah, that was the only way he would address me. He was cold and distant at first, like he was angry to be there."

"Sara, why do you think you managed to escape?" Gray asked.

"I'm a psych major, so I recognized some traits. For starters, he was totally delusional and had this alternate reality playing out in his head. I just went along with it. I think it took him by surprise. I told him how I thought he was the best teacher I ever had and that I was learning so much from him."

"That's interesting," Gray said. "You probably had him questioning his mission, perhaps even starting to rethink his approach. Doing so saved your life."

"I was certain I was meant to be the next biology lesson as soon as he found another student. Why do you think he did what he did?"

"My best guess is that he held a grudge against education institutions. He probably had a traumatic experience as a young boy, perhaps even so far as a bad relationship or experience with a teacher or even other schoolchildren. After hearing what you said, I think teaching these so-called classes was his way of showing others how it should be done, in the most simplistic of ways."

"So he's a crazy psychopath."

"You could say that."

"Did he mention any family or friends?" Sparks asked.

"No. The only people he mentioned were previous students. What will happen now? I mean to Mr. Bowen."

"I guess you aren't aware." Sparks shifted his weight. "He was shot dead last night. You won't have to worry about him again."

Just then, the door opened, and in came Luna's parents.

Sparks, Patton, and Gray cleared out of the room to give the family privacy.

Once outside, Sparks slapped Gray on the back. "I haven't had a chance to officially thank you yet. But I want you to know your thinking and quick action in that cornfield was an integral part of us catching Bowen and saving Luna. I also want to own up and admit I had it wrong with the Howard kid. I'm glad you kept pushing."

"Hey, I'm just happy it worked out the way it did. I wish we could have saved Nia Carter. Is CSI still working the scene?"

"I just got off the phone with the lead investigator, he found a shoebox filled with a bunch of books on Jack the Ripper. Maybe Bowen thought he was the next Ripper."

"Anything else?"

"There was one other thing they found that came across as strange but wasn't sure if it meant anything. They found a handwritten quote on a piece of torn paper in a picture frame that he kept on his dresser. It read 'First one to five gets it all.' It's a little cryptic."

"The Ripper had five confirmed victims. Bowen might have idolized the guy."

"You got a point there."

"What's next for you?" Patton asked. "You heading back to Quantico?"

"Yeah, I spoke to my supervisor this morning. He wants me back as soon as possible. I'm on a flight leaving this afternoon."

"If we ever need the help of the FBI again, you'll be our first call. But I hope that never happens, if you catch my drift."

Gray laughed. "I do."

Later that day, during a taxi ride to the airport, Gray couldn't help but feel a little let down that they weren't able to bring Bowen in alive. Being able to sit down in a room and pick his brain would have been extremely helpful. Not just for Gray, but the other agents in the unit as well. Plus, his finding would have been added to the Violent Criminal Apprehension Program database, or ViCAP.

Nonetheless, Gray was happy that things worked out for Luna. And the man responsible would never be able to do that to another person.

The young woman stirred from her sleep, stretching her legs out while wiggling her toes until they tapped against something strange. That's when she realized she was lying on a hard surface. It was confusing at best because her bed had always been super comfy. She opened her eyes, and harsh fluorescent lighting caused her to squint. As she peeked through her slitted eyelids, she realized she wasn't on her bed. *Why am I on my bedroom floor?* She continued to blink as she used her hands to push herself up into a sitting position. It was only then that she answered her own question. She wasn't in her bedroom. She was in a cage.

19

After touching down at Dulles International Airport a little before five p.m., Gray hired a car to drive him south to Woodbridge, a small town along the Potomac River. He owned a rowhouse there on Rippon Drive, where he had lived for the last three years. It was a quiet neighborhood—families, mostly. It suited Gray, and he had grown comfortable in the community.

Gray exited the black Town Car with his luggage and made his way inside his three-story redbrick-with-white-trim home. Most would think a three-bedroom, three-bath home would be too much house for a single man, but Gray liked the space. He had converted one of the bedrooms into a home office and kept the other as a guestroom. He had no pets, even though he had planned to get a dog as soon as he bought the place. But his work schedule had him continually putting the decision off. It always seemed like it was never a good time.

He was friendly with his neighbors. There was small talk when he came and went. Occasionally, he'd attend a barbecue or grab a beer, but Gray mainly kept to himself outside of that.

Gray grabbed a handful of mail on the way inside. He left his bag at the foot of the stairs in the foyer as he began shuffling through the mail: bills and junk. He walked into the kitchen at the rear of the home and took a beer out of the refrigerator.

Gray's parents had passed. The only family he had was a younger sister, Fleur. She lived in Upstate New York with her husband and two young children. He visited them once a year, at most Video chats had become the norm. There was never a call where Fleur *wouldn't* ask if he was dating anyone. Gray always gave the same answer: "No one that serious."

While in Ames, he'd gotten that breakup email. It was another in a long line of failed attempts at developing a relationship beyond casual dating. The woman in question was Shelly Green.

He had met her at the grocery store; she couldn't reach an item on the highest part of the shelving, and Gray had quickly plucked it down for her. Multiple coffees, lunches and dinners, movies, and walks on the beach, and Green had become the closest thing to a girlfriend that Gray had since he'd been a student at the University of Albany. She'd always joked that if they ever had a child together, Taupe would be a fun name.

Gray plopped down in the leather recliner in the living room and switched on the flat screen with a remote. Before deleting the email from Shelly he had read the part where she said she'd already collected her belongings and would leave the key on the table next to the recliner. Gray glanced over at the key she'd left before he took another sip.

"You're never around. I feel like I'm dating a ghost" was a statement he'd heard increasingly from Shelly during the last couple of months. Gray had done his best to make himself available to her. He actually thought things had gotten better and their relationship had improved. Apparently, it hadn't.

Gray's phone buzzed in his pants pocket. He pulled it out and saw that his supervisor, Phillip Cooper, the Unit Chief at the BAU, had sent him an email. He expected Gray first thing in the morning—a Saturday. Gray wasn't surprised by Cooper's request. He always expected in-person updates as soon as any agent returned from the field. It didn't matter if it was during the workweek or weekend. It was one of the requirements for being a part of the unit.

Before leaving for Iowa, he had discussed getting away for the weekend with Shelly. He'd been terribly busy in the weeks leading up to his trip and wanted to make it up to her. He didn't sense any sort of breakup was coming during that conversation. Still, looking back, he could see there wasn't much enthusiasm on her part. She had already anticipated work getting in the way and wanted to save herself from hearing another excuse.

Gray picked his phone back up and found Green's number. After several rings, he disconnected the call and sent a text message asking if they could talk. He drained the last of his beer while contemplating the rest of his Friday-night plans.

Just then, Green responded to his text, saying she could meet him in the morning at the coffee shop they frequented. She lived roughly fifteen minutes away, and the coffee shop was precisely at the midway point. Gray texted back and asked if they could shift the meeting to late morning. *I guess* was her response.

The following morning Gray woke early and went on his usual three-mile run. He returned home, showered, and caffeinated before making the five-minute walk to the Rippon train station to catch a Virginia Railway Express train. It was an easy eighteen-minute ride to Quantico.

Gray entered the building at the FBI Academy where his offices were located. On Saturday, it was quiet, but Gray knew the commissary was open, so he ducked inside quickly and picked up a breakfast sandwich.

He finished the sandwich on the elevator ride, made his way down the hall to Cooper's office, and poked his head inside.

"Gray, come in. Have a seat. How was your flight back?"

"It was fine," he said as he took a seat.

Cooper's office was standard issue. The only personal items he kept were a few framed pictures on the credenza: his wife and their two daughters. He sat behind his desk, dressed casually and staring at his laptop.

"I'm reading your report right now. You did excellent work over there. Something the higher-ups will be happy to see."

"Thank you."

"I had a few questions regarding the takedown," Cooper said as he looked at his laptop, occasionally glancing up at Gray.

Cooper was always interested in the takedown. He firmly believed not being able to interview a criminal hurt the BAU. He constantly strove to improve his unit's learning.

"You state here that Detective Patton fired the fatal shot."

"That's correct. I was talking to Bowen when he charged at me. That's when Detective Patton took action."

"And you say here Bowen was holding a cleaver." He looked up. "Was it a big one or a small one?"

"Uh, well, it was fairly big. The type a chef in a Chinese restaurant would use to cut up an entire roasted duck."

Cooper nodded. "Where was your service weapon?"

"Bowen had hit me from behind. Upon impact, I lost control of my weapon. I had enough time to regain my feet to face off with him. At that moment, I didn't know where my weapon was."

"I see."

"If Detective Patton had not fired his weapon, in your best estimate, what would have happened?"

"I like to think I would have disarmed Bowen, but to be honest, I could have ended up with a cleaver in my head."

"So you believe Detective Patton did the right thing?"

"I do."

"I agree. It was the right decision."

Gray studied Cooper as he continued to look over the report. It was typical of him to always look for fault. Of course, he knew Cooper saw it as a way to improve, but Gray knew the type. Young and ambitious, some would call it. To Gray, it was more of a get-ahead-by-any-means-possible. Sure, Cooper was intelligent, but he hadn't been in the field that long. He lacked that second sense one develops over time. He was more suited for a desk job and politics. Gray thought Cooper didn't want the BAU to be successful for the greater good, but rather so he could use it as a stepping-stone to his next position. Gray just rolled with it.

Gray spent the next hour fielding questions and essentially reiterating what was already in the report. Afterward, small talk followed to minimize the unspoken directive in the BAU: Work. Work. Work. But it was Saturday, and Gray was in the office. How else should it have felt?

"How's Sheila?" Cooper asked.

"Shelly," Gray responded.

"That's right."

"She's fine. I have plans to meet up with her after I'm finished here."

Cooper looked out of his office window. "It's a nice day. Well, I don't want to hold you up any longer."

And yet you are.

"Go on, get out of here. Enjoy the rest of your weekend. See you bright and early Monday morning."

"I'll see you then," Gray said as he stood. "Enjoy your weekend as well."

20

In the three years that Gray had been based out of Quantico, he hadn't owned a car. He'd been making his way around via public transport or by booking drivers on his phone. He felt the need for a car on rare occasions, but he didn't miss the ownership outside of that. Plus, Green had a car, and she was always okay with taking it so long as he did the driving.

Gray had been dating Green for almost a year. It was a slow start and stayed that way for a while. Green had definitely wanted the relationship to progress quicker. But with Gray's work schedule, it was nearly impossible. He often had to head into the office on the weekend for something, even if it was only for a couple of hours. He'd also begun to travel more during that time. It slowly took its toll on the relationship. Gray hadn't really thought it was that bad until Green sent him the email in Iowa.

His driver came to a stop outside the Black Pot Roasters, a funky little coffee shop where he and Green had their first date. He headed inside, but Green hadn't arrived yet. He ordered a coffee and a cappuccino before taking a seat near the rear of the shop. Green entered a few moments later, and he waved her over.

"Hi, Sterling," Green said as she avoided looking directly into his eyes.

She slung her purse over the back of her chair and sat. He could smell her familiar perfume—something, something, something by Lancôme.

"How was your trip?" she asked, managing a smile.

"Look, Shelly," Gray said, choosing to forgo the small talk. "I know you're angry, and you feel like I haven't been paying enough attention to you or to our relationship. I get it."

"Do you really? Because we've been down this road before, and we've had this talk. I've already heard this reasoning."

Gray drew a heavy breath and grabbed hold of Green's hand. "I need you to understand that my work can be unpredictable and—"

"And I need you to understand that I'm not a dog that'll wag its tail for you when you decide you want attention. You need to make time for me as opposed to seeing me when you have time leftover."

"You're right. I don't dispute what you're saying. All I can say is I'll try and do better, but some things are out of my control. But I will make our relationship a priority. Give us another chance."

Shelly took a sip of her cappuccino. "I can't promise anything."

"I know."

"You'll need to prove yourself over time. I need to see actions, not hear words."

"Absolutely."

"I'm serious, Sterling." This time her hazel eyes looked directly at him. "I don't want to get back on the same merry-go-round. I can't do that."

"A total reboot."

Green breathed deeply. "Okay."

Gray smiled and reached over and gave her thigh a gentle squeeze. "Thank you."

Gray and Green finished their coffee before walking hand in hand to a restaurant farther down the street, where they dined on blue crabs and fresh oysters. Things between the two improved over lunch, which led to a leisurely stroll on the Neabsco Creek Boardwalk. They walked on the scenic trail that cut through the wetlands, playfully hugging and tugging on each other like a couple of teenagers. At six feet, two inches, Gray towered over Green, who barely hung in at five-five. She had an athletic build like Gray. Both had gym memberships and preferred outdoor activities to binge-watching on Netflix.

After their stroll, they picked up groceries, and Gray fixed his famous lasagna back at his place, which they washed down with two bottles of red wine. All in all, what should have been a breakup turned into the start of a healthy recovery.

At about four in the morning, Gray woke from his sleep, breathing heavily. It was the usual reason: the dream. Before becoming an FBI Agent, Gray served in the military: Air Force Pararescue. He had been involved in several operations in the Middle East and Africa. One in particular was responsible for the dream.

Gray and his team had been inserted into Ethiopia, a few clicks away from a small village. They were there to extract a Delta Force team who had been ambushed by a local warlord. Two members of the team were critically injured and needed medical attention fast. They'd been able to make their way out of the hot zone, but they were seriously outnumbered and low on ammunition. It was only a matter of time before the warlord and his men found them. To make matters worse, they were in an area known to have an active lion pride. It was imperative that they be extracted as quickly as possible.

Gray and his team were ordered to parachute under the cover of dark into an area five clicks away from where Delta Force was holed up. Their mission objective was to stabilize the injured and move the Delta Force team to the extraction zone.

Things went sideways from the start.

Through a mix-up of coordinates, Gray and his team were given the wrong location and actually landed three kilometers away from the drop zone, forcing them to cover a greater distance. While there was a drone overhead tracking the warlord's men, the Ethiopian government was unaware of the operation. The last thing the US government wanted was one of their Tomahawk missiles lighting up the local farmland. But Gray wasn't concerned about that. The lions were what had him on edge.

By the time Gray's team had Delta Force in their sights, they were five hours behind schedule. During that time, the warlord's men had discovered Delta Force and were engaging. Gray and his men were able to flank the enemy and drive them back. But it came with a price. Gray had lost a man.

By the time Gray and his team rallied with Delta Force, the two injured men were dead. In addition, Delta Force lost two more men, and the remaining team all had gunshot wounds. Gray couldn't help but feel responsible. Their mistake cost them time. They should have reached Delta Force earlier. They were now saddled with five bodies and a bunch of injured men and in danger of not making it to the extraction zone during the designated window. And the danger of the lions still loomed.

At half a click from the extraction zone, Gray spotted the lions with the help of his thermal imaging optics. The pride was definitely stalking them. When Gray reached the extraction zone, the Black Hawk was still fifteen minutes out and the pride had closed the net around them. Gray didn't want to shoot cats, but if push came to shove, he and his men would have no choice. Gray was seconds from pulling the trigger on a closing lion when the *chuff-chuff-chuff* of a Black Hawk scared the pride off. Gray voluntarily separated from the military shortly after.

"Hey, you okay?" Green asked as she roused from her sleep and rubbed his chest. "Same nightmare?"

"Yeah."

Gray slipped his feet over the side of the bed.

"Where are you going?" Green asked.

"Downstairs. I'll be fine."

"You want me to come with you?"

"Get your rest. I'll have breakfast ready for you when you wake." Gray gave her a peck on her forehead and left.

21

When Monday morning rolled around, Gray woke refreshed and feeling better about his relationship with Green. They'd spent quality time together over the weekend. The playfulness he'd experienced early in their relationship had returned, reminding him that it wasn't often he met someone who connected with him on various levels.

Of course, there was also a lot of talking about expectations. And that was fine with Gray. He liked Green and really wanted things to work out between them. He was well aware that the issues were largely due to him. She'd done nothing wrong. It was up to Gray to make an effort and stick with it. No more "Sorry, I was busy." He needed to make time and put in the work. And he was prepared to do just that.

But when Gray heard his name called in the hallway at the office, he knew the battle would be hard.

"Gray," Cooper called from behind him. "I'm glad I caught up with you. I need you to sit in on a meeting . . ." Cooper looked at his watch. "Fifteen minutes, my office."

"Yeah, sure. Let me grab a coffee and I'll be right in."

When Gray entered Cooper's office, he was already on a video call with people Gray didn't recognize. There were four of them sitting at a conference table, huddled around a camera on their end.

"Ah, here he is," Cooper said. "I'd like you to meet Special Agent Sterling Gray."

"Hello," Gray said. "I apologize for my tardiness."

"Some quick introductions," Cooper said. "Starting from the left side of the table. We have John Holt, DCI Metropolitan Police; next to him is Boyd Hall, DSU Metropolitan Police. That cheery fella is Chi Gaston, DI Metro Police. And last but not least, we have Lillie Pratt. She's a Criminal Intelligence Analyst with Interpol. I hope I got all of that right."

"Quite impressive," Hall said. "Welcome, Special Agent Gray. We appreciate you coming in on this. We are eager to hear your thoughts."

Gray smiled and nodded, not understanding why the Metropolitan Police and Interpol were so eager to meet with him and what he was coming in on. Forget about remembering their names and titles. That went in one ear and out the other. The one thing he was sure of was that he wasn't just there to sit in on a meeting to observe. Those four people looking at him were expecting words to come out of his mouth.

"No problem, but before I get started, could one of you recap the investigation so I can be sure I have all the facts?"

"Well, DI Gaston is the investigator on the case," Hall said. "Best to let him speak."

"Right, then," Gaston said. "A series of connected murders have taken place in London. Three, to be exact. The victims were female, between the ages of twenty-one and twenty-six—of different races. All were put into bin bags and discarded along different motorways."

"Besides age and gender, what were the other connections?" Gray asked.

"Well, the obvious one is the bones."

"Could you expand on that, please?"

"Sorry, yes. Each victim had multiple fractures to their legs, arms, and joints. There was also a severe amount of bruising across the entire body."

"They were badly beaten."

"That's correct."

"The coroner thinks the injuries were caused by a physical assault."

"By some sort of blunt instrument?"

"Yes."

"If I might step in here," Pratt said. "A little background, in case you weren't aware of why we've contacted the FBI. As you may already see, these murders are not typical. We're dealing with a very disturbed person. DI Gaston brought his investigation to my attention in hopes of finding other investigations in the UK or around the world that might have similarities, no matter how tiny."

"You're referring to the investigation I had just worked on. I'm guessing it was the plastic bags that tipped you?"

"That's correct."

"Everyone here has read your report," Hall said. "We all thought it was worth having a chat to see if there was anything you could add that might help us track down the individual responsible."

"I completely understand. I'll be honest, the plastic-bag connection is tiny, but let's put that aside for now. My first instinct is to categorize your suspect as a young white male. He's very angry, not necessarily at the women. It could be a past experience that's triggering him to do what he's doing. Putting the bodies in plastic bags could be his way of conveying they are trash. He discarded them on the side of the road like trash."

"Sorry, you're saying he looks down on women from different races?" Gaston asked.

"It's possible, but it's also possible that it's not related to the women at all. In my previous investigation, our killer filled a plastic bag with the victim's innards. I don't believe this was done to make a point. It was part of the way he cleaned up. And as we later found out, it made absolute sense. Our killer believed he was teaching a human biology class. Cleaning up afterward falls in line with that."

Hall held up his finger. "Sorry, I'll need to put you on mute for just a second."

The video went silent as Gray and Cooper watched them talk briefly with each other before unmuting the video chat.

"Sorry about the wait," Hall said. "Special Agent Gray, if you don't mind, we'd like a quick word with Supervisory Special Agent Cooper."

"No problem."

Gray stood and stepped out of the office into the hallway. He immediately checked his phone as he felt it buzzing in his pants. Green had sent him numerous messages: *I'm thinking about you. Have a nice day. See you this evening.*

Gray took the opportunity to answer her with some equally cute messages. He had just hit the send button when Cooper stuck his head back out the door.

"Gray, come back in, will you?"

Cooper and Gray reconvened in front of the laptop; the other four were still on the video chat.

"The Met team would like you to consult on their investigation," Cooper said. "They believe with your background and the number of successful investigations under your belt, you can help them catch him."

"Of course, I'm happy to help however I can." Gray smiled at the group.

"Great!" Cooper clapped his hands. "It's decided. Special Agent Gray will take the first available flight to London."

22

The Yard, the Metropolitan Police, and the Met are just a few common monikers for law enforcement in London. Gray had always preferred Scotland Yard. It had that cool, Sherlock Holmes vibe about it. Of course, visiting on such short notice wasn't ideal.

Within an hour of Cooper ending the video call with the Metropolitan team, the travel department had booked Gray on a flight to London later that day. Gray had enough time to hurry back to his home, pack, and make it to Dulles for the flight. He texted Green from the airport right before his flight left. She never answered.

Gray touched down at Heathrow International Airport at seven a.m. the next day. He was scheduled to meet Lillie Pratt, the investigator from Interpol, at nine sharp. She would serve as the liaison between him and the folks at the Metropolitan Police.

By the time Gray exited the airport, he only had enough time to take the Tube to New Scotland Yard, where the police headquarters was located. He'd have to check into his hotel later. *Another meet and greet with my luggage in tow.*

The train ride into the city took a little over an hour. Gray spent that time drinking coffee, answering work emails, and staring out the window. The skies were overcast, and the temperature outside was sixty degrees

Fahrenheit. Before leaving Quantico, Gray had discussed his length of stay with Cooper. *Give it a week. Then, we'll see where we're at* was the answer Cooper had given him.

Gray exited the Tube at Embankment Station near Trafalgar Square. From there, it was an eight-minute walk to the Metropolitan Police headquarters. A few seconds after stepping inside the building, Gray heard a woman call his name. He turned and recognized the blond woman approaching him.

"Special Agent Sterling Gray, I'm Lillie Pratt with Interpol," she said with her arm extended. "Welcome to London."

Gray shook her hand. "Thank you, Ms. Pratt. I understand you'll be my liaison while I'm here."

"That's correct. Any questions you have regarding the procedures or whom to speak with at the Metropolitan Police, just let me know and I'll be happy to help you navigate those waters."

"I apologize; I didn't catch which department you worked in at Interpol," Gray said as he looked down at the petite woman dressed in a navy blue pantsuit.

"I'm a Criminal Intelligence Analyst, capable of working on a wide variety of crimes. My role is simple: facilitate investigations."

Gray motioned to the carry-on luggage next to him. "I'm afraid I haven't had time to check in to my hotel. I hope it's not all stairs where we're heading."

"We'll be meeting with the team so you can receive a proper briefing. It shouldn't take long. You can head over to your hotel after."

Pratt led the way to the second floor, where there was an open office plan. Gray recognized DI Chi Gaston sitting at one of the desks. He still had the messy hairdo and five-o'clock shadow he'd noticed during the video call.

"You remember DI Gaston from the call, right?" Pratt asked as they approached.

"Yes, of course," Gray said.

Gaston popped out of his seat and shook hands with Gray. He was short and stocky, something that wasn't apparent during the call.

"Special Agent Gray. I'm glad you were able to come out here."

"Please, there's no need to address me in a formal matter. You both can call me Sterling."

"Bloody hell, am I happy to hear that. I can't stand titles. Call me Chi." Gaston looked at Lillie. "What do you say, Ms. Pratt?"

"Lillie is fine."

"Now that we got that out of the way, let's turn our attention to the board."

Behind Gaston's desk was a standing bulletin board. Pinned to it were crime scene photos, a map of London with the location of the bodies noted, various names with a question mark after them, and other information that Gaston had collected to date. Gaston quickly walked Gray through the investigation, which was a nice reminder.

"So, three bodies so far. Any missing persons as of late that could be tied to this?" Gray asked.

"If there are others, I haven't been able to make the connection. Three days is the time frame from when these women were reported missing to when their bodies were discovered. According to the coroner, the time of death was about twenty-four hours before the bodies were discovered."

"So, safe to say he's keeping them alive for at least a couple of days," Gray said.

Gaston nodded. "During our earlier call, you mentioned anger could be fueling our killer. Do you think he gets angrier over time and then ends up killing the women because of that? It seems like if he's angry at them, he would kill them right off."

"There is truth to that last statement, but let me clarify a bit. His anger may not be related to the women. In fact, I don't think it is. His anger is most likely the result of a past experience. Much like the killer back in Iowa, these types of people often use victims as a way to make a point, like a tool."

"Bloody messed-up way to make a point." Gaston let out a long breath as he rested his hands on his waist.

Gray stepped closer to the board to better look at the plastic bags the women were stuffed inside of before being discarded. "Was there any writing on the bags?"

"What do you mean?"

"Did the killer write a message or a note on them with a marker?"

Gaston shook his head. "But I can double-check, though. Why?"

"The killer in Iowa made notes on the bags. Really, I'm just thinking out loud. The best way forward right now is to take a closer look at any missing-person reports over the last two days. Besides sex, age, and the victims being of color did you come across anything else to connect them? Did they work in the same profession or live in the same area of London?"

"No similarities with work or residences. I looked through their social media and didn't see any friend connections or interest in similar events. There was one thing that connected two of the victims. They were members at the same gym. It's a chain and popular place, so a lot of people go there."

"Anything come out of that?"

"When I spoke to the staff at reception, none of them recalled seeing the women, but a check of their records showed one victim always took a Zumba class. The other one didn't. One came after work. The other preferred visiting in the morning, before work."

"I'd like to visit the most recent crime scene and that gym. It'll help put me in the killer's mindset."

23

The young man was dressed in a black athletic shirt and shorts and carried a metal canister filled with water. He'd just finished fifteen minutes of stretching and had started on fifteen minutes of skipping rope. It was the middle of the day during the week, so the gym wasn't very crowded during his midday workout. He'd been training at the UK-based gym for only two months. Most days, he'd come to the gym three times a day.

His morning workout consisted of cardio and a boxing class when available. Midday was reserved for cardio and strength training. And in the evening, he joined one of the new mixed martial arts training classes.

Before joining, he spent a few years training alone and with personal trainers at gyms geared toward mostly MMA. When he was younger, he made the rounds at various strip-mall dojos. Even though some of the MMA classes at the gym were labeled 'advanced,' they were still designed for and aimed at the mass of office workers that descended on the place. No one would walk out of those classes with the conditioning or skill set of a competitive fighter. It was akin to the trendy strip-pole cardio classes—be stripper-like without being a stripper.

He mainly kept to himself during his workouts, often switching things up so that he wasn't around others. If too many people were using the free weights, he'd settle for pushups, lunges, and sit-ups. He wasn't interested in small talk or grabbing a pint. In fact, he couldn't stand the people that came to the gym, primarily the gym rats—the ones who were there just as much as he was. Posers. That's what he thought of the bunch. If they were serious, they wouldn't train at the gym that made most of their money at the start of the year when enthusiastic people plunked down a crapload of money on binding contracts to fulfill their new year's resolutions only to bail on the effort after a week or two.

Giving a quick shake to the metal container he had filled with water and powered electrolytes, he took a few gulps. He had thirty minutes left on his strength-training routine. *Come on. Stop thinking about getting back home and get through this workout. Nothing will change during that time.*

Biceps, shoulders, and a quick abdominal workout ate up the time quicker than he expected. He collected his belongings from the locker room and headed back home.

The man lived alone in a two-bedroom home about a ten-minute drive north of Hyde Park in Maida Vale. He was self-employed as a cryptocurrency trader and worked from home. Aside from his daily training, he enjoyed teaching others how to stop slaving away at a nine-to-five job and work for themselves by investing in cryptocurrency.

He didn't give structured classes. They were really just meetups at a local coffee shop or pub. Very low-key. There, he would provide people with a quick overview of what trading was like. If they were interested, he'd meet with them again and offer more advice—women only, though. He never accepted appointments with men. Women were the ones who really needed his help. And they didn't question him like men did. He couldn't stand it when someone asked his advice, no matter how polite they were about it.

As soon as he entered his home, he headed into the kitchen and heated up the leftover lasagna he had purchased the day before. After wolfing down the food, along with a post-workout shake, he took a quick shower and changed into something more appropriate for a class he would be teaching soon.

He then took the stairs to the basement, where he unlocked the door and entered a small room. He flipped the light switch and the room lit up. The walls and floors were covered entirely in white EVA foam mats, the type typically found in gyms where wrestling or gymnastics took place. In the corner stood a water cooler, and a whiteboard hung on one of the walls.

Using a dry-erase marker, he wrote on the whiteboard: *Welcome to Mixed Martial Arts.* He capped the pen and then slipped on black latex gloves.

He turned around and faced a dog kennel at the rear of the room. Sitting inside was a young woman, visibly shaking as she held her knees up against her chest.

"In my class, you will address me as Sensei and only as Sensei. You are my student. Are you clear?"

The woman said nothing.

"Student, I asked if you were clear."

She nodded her head.

"Good. Are you ready for your first lesson?"

"What lesson? What are you talking about?" she asked with a shaky voice.

The man unlocked the cage door and yanked the woman out. She lay sprawled across the mats on her stomach. As she got up on her hands and knees, he jumped on top of her, knocking her back down. He quickly hooked a leg around her belly, pulled back, and flipped her over so that she was lying with her back on top of him. He grabbed hold of her left wrist.

"You see how I have control of your left wrist? I'll move my right leg so that my knee is positioned under the armpit of your right arm. See how that limits your motion. You can't roll away. Do you understand, Student?"

"Yes, I understand. Please, don't hurt me."

"You shouldn't feel any pain. I'm not applying pressure. I'm just showing you how a person can defend from an attack if they are on their back and their opponent is on top of them. You're on top of me. I'm on my back. So first, I immobilize you. Your movement is limited, is it not?"

She nodded.

"Now I'm gripping your left wrist with my right hand, correct?"

"Yes."

"I then reach under your arm with my left hand and grip my wrist, creating a kimura, or a double joint arm lock. Now I will release my knee from under your right armpit and roll out from under you while lifting my right leg up and placing it over your chest and locking it down across your throat. I now have one leg across your neck and one across your belly, pinning you down against the mat. Are you clear so far, Student?"

The woman started to cry uncontrollably.

"There's no need to be afraid. You are not in any pain at the moment. Remain calm and pay attention. Now I will slowly lean back and extend your left arm so it's straight and flat against my body. Just like this. You see? No pain, right?"

She nodded.

"This submission is called a straight arm bar. No pain, right? But if I hook my left arm around yours, like I'm choking you, even the slightest pressure will cause pain in your elbow."

The girl screamed, and the man released the pressure.

"You see how super powerful this submission is? Slight pressure caused you to cry out in pain. So you can imagine if more force was used on your opponent, how quickly they would submit. If they don't submit, this is what happens."

Crack!

The woman screamed in pain.

"That was your elbow joint snapping. Your right arm is now useless. Let's move on to the next lesson."

24

After the briefing with Gaston, Gray was eager to get to work and decided not to drop off his luggage at the hotel just yet. Instead, he stored it next to Gaston's desk, and the three left the building.

The gym Gaston had mentioned was called Fitness World, and they had close to three hundred locations throughout the UK. They touted themselves as everyone's gym.

"There are three within a thirty-minute walk from the Met," Gaston said as they exited the building. "The location our victims visited is about a twenty-minute walk, if you two don't mind, only a straight shot west along Victoria Street."

Gray and Pratt shook their heads.

"Chi, do investigators here normally work cases by themselves?" Gray asked.

"No. We usually have a team, but we're stretched thin at the moment. The higher-ups didn't realize this case would blow up into something much larger. It's why the fine people at Interpol and the FBI are involved. This situation can run out of control quickly, especially if the media learns that the victims are connected. That information has been suppressed. Every time the media hears about a possible serial killer, Jack the Ripper comparisons flood the news channels, and people's imaginations get the best of them. The last thing I want is panic in the city."

Gray understood Gaston's concern. Avoiding media attention was critical. Some killers craved attention. Others simply didn't realize they wanted it until they had it. By then, it was too late.

A short walk later, the group approached a three-story building with a glass facade. Gray noticed exercise bikes and treadmills lining the window on the second floor. Just inside the building, a spunky young woman dressed in black leggings with a matching crop top sat the reception desk.

"Hi, welcome to Fitness World," she said with a bright smile. "Are you ready to start your path to a healthy life?"

Gaston produced his identification. "I'm DI Gaston. Is it possible to speak to the manager on duty?"

"Oh, okay. Just a minute, please."

The woman made a phone call and then let Gaston know that her manager would be out in a few seconds. Gray's attention had been on a personal trainer helping a client stretch. Just beyond them were several different chrome fitness machines.

A man dressed in black athletic apparel appeared from a door behind the reception desk a few moments later. "Hello. I'm Harry Davies, the manager on duty. How can I be of help?"

"Mr. Davies, I'm DI Gaston. These are my colleagues. I believe I spoke to you once before."

"Yes, you're right. I remember now."

"I have additional questions, if that's all right?"

"Uh, sure. Is there a problem?"

"No problem, just gathering more information."

He nodded. "Come back to the office."

Once settled into the small office, Gaston produced two names. "Last time we spoke about two members: Ava Kwan and Emily Wokomo." Gaston didn't feel the need to inform Davies that the women were deceased.

"Yes, I remember. Let me look up their information." Davies typed on the laptop sitting on his desk.

"Okay. Both Ava and Emily are current on their memberships, but it doesn't look like either one has been in here recently. It's been a couple of weeks."

"Did either woman sign up with one of your personal trainers?" Gray asked.

Davies squinted as he looked at his laptop. "Um, Ava did take advantage of our free personal trainer offer. Emily did not."

"And what does that consist of?".

"A full hour with one of our trainers. They discuss the client's goals and how they can go about achieving them. They also teach exercises to help our clients get started on that path."

"Is that trainer still employed here?" Gaston quickly asked.

"Yes, of course. She is one of our most popular trainers."

"Might be a good idea to ask her a few questions. Is she in today?"

"I'm afraid not. She took two days off … Family issues."

"If you don't mind, could you provide us with a number so we can follow up with her?"

"Yes, of course."

"How long were Ava and Emily members at the gym?" Gray asked.

"They're fairly new. Both signed up two months ago. They are what we consider casual members. These members usually visit three times per week for an hour."

"In your experience, would an absence of two weeks tell you that member has decided to stop coming?"

"No, not at all. Sometimes people get busy. If it carries on for more than a month, then I would agree with your statement. Did something happen to them?"

"Nothing for you to be concerned about, really just gathering information," Gaston said. "Do you mind if we have a look around?"

"Be my guest. I can escort you and answer any questions you might have, if you want."

"I think we'll be okay on our own."

Davies walked them back to the reception area. "If you need anything else, I'll be here all day."

"You weren't kidding about the media. Even Davies doesn't know those two women aren't coming back," Gray said as they walked around the first floor.

Gaston shrugged. "Normally, I would have informed him, but with the nature of this crime and his lack of knowing anything concrete about these two women, there was no need to bring him into it. Still isn't."

"It's a long shot, but talking to the trainer might lead somewhere," Pratt said.

"Sure. I don't want to overlook any detail," Gaston answered. "Sterling, anything useful come to mind?"

"You mentioned earlier one of the victims came in the morning and the other at night."

"That's correct."

"If our guy was watching them, he's most likely a gym rat. He comes in multiple times a day. Maybe Davies can pull a list of names of members in the last two months who come here more than once a day. Also, I'm not so sure we can rule out staff. They're here all day as well. There might be a pattern of certain staff members here on the days that our victims came in."

"Good idea," Gaston said. "Excuse me. I'll make that request right now with Davies."

Gray and Pratt headed up to the second floor.

"Do you have a gym membership?" she asked as they walked along a row of stationary bikes.

"I do have one. And I'm guilty of being one of those three-times-a-week people."

"Same here. It takes a fair amount of commitment just to do that." Pratt stopped midstep. "I sense you don't believe the gym has any connection to the investigation except that two of our victims were members."

"Eh, I'm not ruling this place out, but I am trying to wrap my mind around the killer's motivation. He's definitely angry, but what I'm trying to determine is the source of that anger. A short fuse isn't normally the trigger for someone to repeatedly kill that way."

25

A car was needed to get to the crime scene of the latest victim. Gaston suggested they head back to the station and take his car.

"Whereabouts are you staying?" Gaston asked Gray as they made the walk back.

"I believe it's called the Trafalgar Hotel."

"Bloody fancy place they have you at," he said. "The FBI takes care of the agents overseas very well."

"It must be a mistake, because I'm used to staying in rooms with thin walls and vending machines in the hallway," Gray said with a smile.

"It's walking distance from the station," Gaston said. "Eight minutes."

"Great. I'll check in, drop off my luggage, and we can hit the road."

Once back at the station, Gray grabbed his luggage and made the short trek to the Trafalgar. His room was ready, so he headed up and took an opportunity to freshen up and replace the suit with jeans, a button-down, and a light jacket.

One condition of helping the Metropolitan Police: he wasn't allowed to carry a firearm. Most police officers in the UK are unarmed anyway. Gray wasn't there on the authority to investigate a crime and make an arrest. Much like Pratt, he was there to help facilitate the investigation—more precisely, to work up a profile on the killer. It was up to Gaston to catch him. But lines do blur.

Gray grabbed a coffee from a kiosk and drank it on his way to headquarters. He hadn't eaten anything since the small meal he was fed on the plane, and his hunger pangs were growing. Pratt was on her phone outside the entrance to the station when he arrived, so Gray hung around and worked on his cup of coffee.

"Sorry," she said, disconnecting the call. "Chi is bringing the car around."

"Have you had anything to eat today?" Gray asked.

"Breakfast in the morning, but I could go for a bite." She glanced at her watch. "It's about that time."

"We'll ask Chi and see if he's feeling hungry," Gray said. "Maybe we can stop somewhere on the way to the crime scene. If I recall correctly, Interpol's headquarters are in Manchester. Do you work out of that office?"

"Interpol has a satellite office here. A few others and I work from there."

"Does assisting the Metropolitan Police make up most of your workload?"

"I've worked with Chi on a number of investigations over the years, but it doesn't monopolize my time. The unit I work in can be pulled into almost any investigation around the world. So travel is a large part of my job, which I like but dread at times."

"I know what you're saying. The opportunities to work on different investigations make the job very interesting. Still, being on the road . . . It has its drawbacks."

"If you don't mind me asking, how long have you worked in the BAU?"

"I've been a BAU analyst for just under five years."

"And before the FBI?"

"Military."

"Let me guess, Special Forces?" Pratt said with a smile.

"You're right. Pararescue—Air Force. How did you know?"

"The way you carry yourself . . . and your haircut."

Gray ran a hand over his buzz cut. "Old habits die hard."

"My father is ex-SAS."

"Ah, a fine group as well. I hear they're letting women apply to the SAS," Gray said.

"They are, but that's not my cup of tea. I like the work I do with Interpol. I'm a techno nerd."

"Funny, you don't look like a nerd."

"That's my special weapon," Pratt said with a wink.

"Then I'm glad you're part of the team."

A horn honked, grabbing Gray's and Pratt's attention. Parked at the curb in front of them was a silver Ford Fiesta. Gaston shouted for them to get inside.

"Chi, how do you feel about a lunch?" Gray asked.

"I'm not opposed to eating. I know a great pub on the way out there. Excellent food."

"Sounds great," Gray said.

About thirty minutes later, Chi pulled off of the M4 motorway. A couple of lefts and rights, and he parked outside a pub named The Hounds.

"My mouth's already watering," Chi said as he climbed out of the driver's seat. "It's been ages since I've been here. They have a great pie and mash."

The three filed into the pub and grabbed a cozy table in the corner.

"I recommend the pie and mash, but you can't go wrong with fish and chips," Chi said as he looked over the menu.

"That's what I'll have, the fish and chips," Gray said. "Lillie, do you have a favorite at the pub?"

"I think I'll have the steak and chips."

"Right, then, I'll put the order in at the bar. Fancy a round of pints?"

"Why not? When in Rome," Gray said.

"Sterling, have you tried cask ale?" Chi asked.

"I have, actually, and I liked it. It's been a while, and I can't remember the name."

"I'll take a pint of London Pride," Pratt said.

"That's the name of the beer I tried," Gray said as he snapped his finger. "I'll have a pint of that."

Chi left to place the order.

"This might sound silly, but I have to ask. Have you been to the UK before?" Pratt asked.

"Yes, but it was many years ago, and I was just passing through on my way back to the States. But it's great being back here. And you, have you traveled to the US much?"

"A few times—always on business. I do wish to have a proper holiday. San Francisco is on the list, followed by Chicago, only because all of my previous visits were to New York."

"New York is a great city. Can't go wrong there."

"It's lovely, but it's not the same when you're there to work."

Gray held his hands up. "No argument from me."

Chi returned with three pints filled with deep golden amber ale topped with a nice head. He held up his pint. "Here's to us catching this bloody bastard."

"Cheers," Gray and Pratt said in unison as they clinked their glasses together.

"Chi, how long have you been with the Met?" Gray asked.

"It's the only career I've ever known. When I got out of uni, I was set on being a squaddie with Her Majesty's Armed Forces, but a friend talked me into being a bobby. Don't ask me why, but it made sense at the time. Looking back, I think I'm better suited as a detective. I like the problem-solving aspect of it."

"I get it. That's also what drew me into the FBI," Gray said.

"Sterling's background is Special Forces—Pararescue," Pratt said.

"No way? Makes sense. You're swooping in here to save the day," Chi said with a chuckle

"The day isn't saved yet."

Gaston and Pratt laughed as Gray held up his glass.

"Here's to teamwork because we all know that's how real police work is done."

The three enjoyed their meals over lively conversation. An hour felt like fifteen minutes. But as soon as the forks were down and the last of the ale had been drained, they were back on the road.

It took another thirty minutes to reach the location. Gaston pulled off the side of the busy highway and brought his car to a stop.

"This is it," he said, pointing to a tree line about ten feet away. "He couldn't even be bothered to drag the victim a few feet farther, where it would have been completely hidden from view."

"You weren't kidding when you said he discarded the body off the side of the highway. Two victims back in Iowa were left on the side of the road next to a cornfield."

"Plastic bags and body disposal are two similarities," Pratt said. "Could that say something about our killer? Is he the same as Gary Bowen?" she asked as they followed Gaston.

"In the general sense, I would say he is, but I need to learn more to really get a solid grasp of who he is."

"This is the spot," Gaston pointed at the ground. "A road crew just happened to be collecting rubbish on the side of the highway when they came across the bin bag that held Kwan's body. It would have taken longer to discover her if it weren't for them."

Gray rested his hands on his waist as he looked around at the passing vehicles. "Is it just as busy at night?"

"It calms down a little, but this is a major highway heading out of London, so there's always a good amount of traffic."

"Any CCTV coverage along this section of the highway?" Gray asked.

"There is quite a bit of coverage, just not in this area. This chap might have known that and picked this spot on purpose."

"It's possible," Gray said, "but to know that, he would have to be a frequent commuter on this highway. And even then, how many commuters really pay attention to that. I'd place money on him doing his homework. But if that really is the case, he would have known dumping the bag a few feet farther back and in the trees would have provided all the coverage he needed. I think he pulled over, tossed the bag out, and quickly got out of here. He got lucky."

"I still gravitate toward the similarities," Pratt said.

"I already know where you're heading." Gray looked over at her. "It's not the same guy. Bowen's dead. But hey, we're paid to overthink, right?"

26

Gaston asked if Gray had wanted to visit the other two crime scenes of the earlier victims, but he declined, stating the photos were enough. The ride back to the station was a mixture of both work and personal related conversation. Gray talked about being a people watcher since he was a little boy. The way people interacted with others had always held his interest. Pratt and Gaston didn't disappoint.

"My father's side of the family is originally from the south of France," Gaston said.

"Law enforcement?" Gray asked.

"Not even close. They were fromagers, or cheesemakers, if you prefer."

"Really? I've never met a family of cheesemakers," Gray said. He turned to look at Pratt, who was sitting in the back seat. "Can you top that?"

"How about a family of stalkers?"

"Huh?"

"It's what we Brits call deer hunters."

"You bagged a deer yourself?"

"I have. I even know how to field dress. My father loved venison. It was very common on the supper table while growing up."

A smile formed on Gray's face. "Look at you two. I'm thoroughly impressed, and a bit embarrassed that I don't have an equally impressive story to tell. But, Lillie, I'll agree with you: venison is tasty."

"You're a fan, are you?"

"When I was serving in the military, one of the fellas I knew received dried venison in his care packages."

"If you're interested, I know a great restaurant in the city that serves quality game."

"Are you talking about the Black Forest?" Gaston asked.

"Yes, have you been?"

"Once. If Lillie is offering to take you, I'd say accept the invitation. You'll love it."

"Well, in that case, how about tonight? Will that work for you?" Gray suggested.

"Sure, if you don't mind an early supper."

"I don't mind at all. Gaston, are you game as well?"

"Sorry, mate. My daughter has a school function this evening. She has a bit part in a play."

"That's certainly not something you can miss. Another time."

"Was there anything else you wanted to see today regarding the investigation?" Gaston asked.

"I think I've seen enough. I would love some time alone to begin working on a profile, if that's okay."

"You'll get no complaints from me," Gaston said.

"Lillie, is it all right if we meet at the restaurant?" Gray asked.

"That's fine. I'll text you the information."

After returning to the station, Gray made the short walk back to his hotel. He was eager to start working up a profile on Gaston's unsub. It would be a work in progress, but one had to start somewhere.

Entering the grand lobby of the Trafalgar reminded Gray of Gaston's earlier comment about being put up in a nice place. Gray didn't get it either. Usually, he booked himself into a midrange, no-frills hotel. But this time, Cooper's assistant handled the arrangements. *Did she just normally do what she would have done for Cooper? If so, that man traveled well.* Gray certainly wasn't complaining.

In his room, Gray cracked open a bottle of sparkling water from the mini fridge and got to work. The first thing he did was clear the mind of his previous investigation. He didn't want it to skew his thinking. *Just the facts, Gray. Rely on what you've learned so far.*

One thing had popped into Gray's head during the day. And that was the connection to the gym that Gaston was trying to make. It made complete sense and was probably his strongest lead. When Gray mentioned that it made sense, he spied a twinkle in Gaston's eyes. Was it hope that someone besides him, someone with fresh eyes on the case, thought there could be a connection to the gym? Perhaps. Gray certainly wasn't discounting it, but his gut wasn't going gangbusters when he visited. No concrete reason why. He just felt lukewarm about the prospects.

Our killer may frequent the gym, and he might have noticed his victims there. But abducting them from there? I don't see it happening. Too many people. A ton of foot traffic outside. At the very least, he'd have to lure them somewhere else.

Gray started his list.

- *White male between ages of 22 and 30.*
- *Self-employed or unemployed.*
- *Lives in the city—owns or has access to a vehicle.*
- *He's angry, possibly a control freak.*
- *Physical trauma suggests he's taking his anger out on them, perhaps using them as an example.*
- *Discarding the bodies in plastic bags could suggest the victims are worthless.*
- *Either mission-oriented or power-control driven.*

Gray couldn't yet determine which of those two categories the killer fell into, but he was reasonably sure that he was one or the other, possibly a little of both.

As he continued to think about what was driving this person to kill, Gary Bowen popped back into his head. Bowen's true motivation was to rid society of a flawed educational system in an unconventional and highly illogical way. But killing those women did nothing to punish those he believed to be in the wrong. Instead, it only further victimized the people he had tried to protect. He'd chosen the wrong solution to a problem he'd concocted in his head. Could the same thing be at play here? Could this killer be doing the same?

This guy isn't organized. An organized killer would have done a much better job of disposing of the bodies. But at the same time, the victims are not random, even though he wants it to appear that way. I'm not buying it. The gym is proof that he had spent time watching at least two of his victims. He may have more than one location to source his victims.

As Gray continued to work, Bowen stuck in his head like an annoying pop song that he just couldn't stop humming.

Wait a minute, pal. Why are you making comparisons? These are two separate cases. So what if the plastic bag was the reason you were brought in? Forget about Bowen. Forget about how and why he killed. Forget about Iowa completely.

But no matter how much Gray tried to focus on the facts of the current investigation, Bowen remained in his thoughts.

Okay, let's assume these two killers are alike. Then that would mean Gaston's unsub is trying to right a wrong, and the killings are not about power or control. Something traumatic happened to him earlier in life, and he's holding a grudge. So what would he be trying to convey by beating a young woman to death? And not just a regular beating—he literally snapped their bones. The medical examiner's report suggested a blunt object was responsible but couldn't get any more specific.

Gray pulled up photos of the victims' bodies on his laptop.

It doesn't look like someone used a bat on these women. I've also seen my fair share of snapped arms and legs. A bat or a pipe doesn't inflict damage like that. It's almost as if they were caused by someone using physical force, like a nasty domestic violence case. The medical examiner should have picked up on that.

Just then, Gray had a flashback to the gym when he saw the trainer on the floor mat helping his client stretch. *I wonder . . .*

Gray did an online search for the gym. After locating the website, he checked to see what classes they had to offer. *Well, I'll be damned.* The gym offered beginner mixed martial arts classes. From the description, the class was pretty tame. It seemed to focus primarily on conditioning. But the advanced class did offer some training in grappling.

Someone teaching this class would easily know how to apply pressure in the right place to snap a forearm or pop a shoulder out of its socket. Maybe Gaston was right about the gym. Maybe the person teaching that class is a person of interest.

27

Gray received a message from Pratt to meet at the Black Forest at six p.m. He grabbed a quick shower and changed into fresh jeans, a button-down, and a leather jacket. He had packed a bottle of cologne out of habit, but he rarely used it. But today, he gave himself two shots.

Gray, what the hell are you doing? Lillie is your colleague.

If you haven't noticed, she's really pretty.

You need to keep it professional.

But it seemed like she was flirting a bit.

She was nice to you.

Maybe.

Don't forget about Shelly back home.

She hasn't answered any of my text messages.

Let her calm down. Give her some time.

Gray did himself a favor and took his own advice. Pratt was a colleague, and she deserved the respect of being treated like one. On the other hand, Gray knew the reality with Shelly and struggled to keep a doomed relationship afloat. As much as he wanted to make things work with her, he knew where that ship was heading.

The Black Forest was located in the Chelsea neighborhood on Kings Road. A bit farther than Gray felt like walking, so he grabbed a cab. Ten minutes later, he stood outside a Tudor restaurant that looked like it was straight from one of Grimms' fairy tales. He was five minutes early. So was Pratt.

"Sterling," a woman's voice called out.

He spun around saw Pratt walking toward him. She had changed out of her business suit and into a chic outfit that made her smile pop even brighter.

"Hi, Lillie."

"I hope you're hungry," she said.

"Always."

Gray picked up on her perfume as he followed her into the restaurant. He hadn't noticed it earlier and wondered if she'd put it on just for their dinner.

The inside of the restaurant resembled a hunter's cabin with the heads of big game mounted on the walls. In addition to the heads, there were also animal skins, rifles, and photographs of hunters. The smell of grilled meat filled the air. For an early dinner, there were quite a few people already dining. Gray looked at the dishes on the tables as they walked past, and his mouth watered.

"Do you eat here often?" he asked as they were escorted to a table.

"Maybe two or three times a year," she said as she sat.

"Pretty cool place, and from what I can see, the food looks delicious." Gray picked up the menu. "They have quite a few venison dishes here. Do you have a recommendation?"

"The braised venison shanks are perfect. You'll love them. But I also recommend the pan-roasted fillets with a side of shepherd's pie. It's absolutely delightful. The pie is served in a cute little tin."

"They both sound great. This will be a hard choice."

"I always face the same dilemma when I come here. If you're up for it, I can order one dish, and you can order the other, and we can share."

"That sounds perfect," Gray said. "Is it too much to suggest a nice bottle of red to wash it down?"

"Not at all. A nice cabernet will do just fine."

After placing their order, Pratt asked how the profile was coming along.

"It's always a work in progress, but I'll bullet point it for you. A white male between the ages of twenty-two and thirty. He has some higher education. He lives in the city but has access to a vehicle. He is either self-employed or unemployed. Because of the degree of physical trauma, I still believe he's angry, but that anger is rooted in a past experience. He has control issues, a very dominating personality. An interesting thought I did have ties back to the gym. The medical examiner's report said the injuries were the result of some sort of blunt object. But some of the injuries appear to have been made by a person."

"Bare hands?"

"Yes. Are you familiar with MMA, mixed martial arts?"

"I know of it."

"So there are a lot of moves that, when done properly, can easily snap a bone in half."

"So you think our killer is an MMA enthusiast and is practicing on these women."

"I agree with the first part of your statement. I'm not quite sure if it's practice or rage."

"You think he knew these women personally?"

"Not on a personal level, just whatever he gathered from watching them. The interesting thing is that Fitness World offers MMA classes. Not anything serious; conditioning, really."

"Our unsub could possibly be an instructor there?"

"Correct. It should be looked into by Chi."

"Why do I hear a 'but' coming?"

"Because I'm not entirely convinced it's an instructor. The problem is the abduction. There's too much foot traffic both inside and outside. If anything, I lean toward another member."

"But if he works there, he could have access to a member's personal information, like where they live."

"That's right, and that's why I think Chi still needs to look into it. I think it's possible our guy is meeting the women at the gym, not necessarily in these classes, and then making arrangements to meet elsewhere. The classes are strictly for his enjoyment."

"I'm not sure how you got there, but it's definitely an interesting approach."

"A profile isn't always a direct road map. Nothing is guaranteed. A big part of me making the leap is due to my gut and my lifelong observation of human nature."

Just then, the server returned with a bottle of wine and poured two glasses.

Pratt lifted her glass. "Here's to your gut being right."

Gray couldn't help but notice throughout dinner how easy conversation came. It actually reminded him of his time spent with Shelly. The only difference was that Pratt worked in law enforcement. She knew how hectic and unpredictable their schedules could be. Dating a woman like Pratt would essentially erase a lot of his and Green's problems. Of course, Gray wasn't thinking of dating Pratt. He was simply noting the possibilities of dating a woman like Pratt.

"Dinner was amazing," Gray said, placing his cloth napkin on the table.

"Was the meal the only thing you enjoyed?"

Gray smiled. "The company was equally amazing as well."

"Thank you. I had a wonderful time myself."

Gray then offered to pick up the check.

"You don't have to do that," Pratt said. "We'll split it down the middle."

"The bureau is paying for this dinner. Interpol can pay for the next one."

After taking care of the bill, Gray and Pratt headed out of the restaurant. The sidewalks were still busy with people either making their way home or grabbing a bite to eat. Gray glanced at his watch. It was seven thirty p.m. The night was young, and since they'd been enjoying each other's company, he thought about asking Pratt if she was interested in having a drink at one of the nearby pubs. Before he could open his mouth, she opened hers.

"What are your plans for the rest of the evening?"

"Unless we get a nightcap, I'll probably just head back to my hotel."

Pratt moved in a bit closer and looked up at Gray. "Are you telling me you aren't tired of my company?" She playfully tapped on his chest.

Okay, if that's not flirting, I don't know what is. Gray smiled at her. "Not by a long shot. How about another drink at that pub over there?"

Pratt glanced quickly over her shoulder before focusing back on Gray and scrunching her nose. "Oh, I'm sorry. My ride will be here any minute."

"Your ride? Don't tell me you have a driver?"

"I do."

"Fair enough. Next time, Interpol will definitely pick up the check."

"I will," Pratt said as she stared directly into Gray's eyes.

Wow, is this an invitation for a good-night kiss? You better be sure, Gray. It'll go horribly wrong if it's not. But hey, you only live once, right? Just go for it.

While Gray mulled making a move, someone called Pratt's name. Gray and Pratt both looked toward the direction of the voice and saw a woman sitting in the driver's seat of a car.

"Lillie!" The woman waved.

"That's my ride," Pratt said.

"Is that a friend?" Gray asked.

"No, silly. That's my wife, Evie. She's a nurse at the hospital. We finally got a night where our work schedules freed both of us up. Sort of. She scheduled for the late shift tonight." Pratt ushered Gray over to the car. "Evie, this is Special Agent Sterling Gray, the one who crossed the pond to help out on an investigation."

"Nice to meet you, Sterling," Evie said. "Welcome to London."

"Well, we must be off," Pratt said as she opened the passenger door, "but I'll see you tomorrow morning at headquarters."

"Yes, you will. Have a good night. Nice meeting you, Evie." Gray waved.

"Cheers!" Evie said.

Gray watched Pratt climb into the passenger seat and give Evie a kiss on the lips. He couldn't help but think he had just dodged a major bullet. *Sheesh, Gray. You can profile a person you never met right down to a tee, but when it comes figuring out a woman, you're not even in the ballpark.*

28

The following day, the young man arrived at the Cuppa coffee shop a little before seven thirty a.m. It was the first time he'd visited that particular one, indulging the request of the woman he was meeting. He ordered hot tea with milk, took a seat at a table away from the other patrons in the shop, and buried his head in a newspaper. Ten minutes later, a woman tapped him on the shoulder.

"Hi," she said. "I'm Evie. Are you Eddie?"

"Yes, I'm Eddie."

"I'm sorry I'm late. Work was a madhouse."

"Not a problem. I just arrived myself. Did you want to get a hot tea or something before we start?"

She pulled out a metal canister from her purse as she sat. "I already have some. Thank you so much for meeting me on such short notice."

"Quite all right. I have a flexible schedule." He smiled at her. "What sort of work do you do?"

"I'm a nurse. I love it, but the hours are brutal. I just finished the night shift."

"Well, hopefully one day, you'll have the same flexible schedule that I have."

"That would be perfect. To leave the rat race and work at home." Evie stared off into the distance momentarily before looking back at Eddie.

"Let me first start by saying this. Buying and selling cryptocurrencies do come with risks. It's very easy to lose money. So I tell everyone to only spend what they are comfortable losing. But the upside is tremendous. You'll most likely make what you lost back and much more."

"Have you lost a lot of money?"

"I have. Once I lost seventy-five thousand pounds in a few hours."

"Oh my God! What did you do?"

"My initial investment was ten thousand pounds. I was able to turn that into one hundred and fifty thousand pounds. Even though I lost seventy-five, I was still up. In fact, I had already taken my initial investment out. Anyway, I took whatever free money I had and bought an additional twenty thousand pounds at the lower price. The currency recovered, and I made the seventy-five thousand I had lost back and much, much more."

"Brilliant. That's what I want."

Eddie pulled out his laptop, and for the next thirty minutes, he gave Evie a beginner's overview of cryptocurrency trading. She listened, occasionally asking for clarification during his presentation.

"What do you think? Are you still interested?" Eddie asked.

"Absolutely. With a small investment. I can easily monitor my holdings with my phone while I'm at work."

"Of course you can. Once your profits are enough, you can withdraw your initial investment. That way, you never lose the money you originally had, only profit."

"I'm sold. I definitely want to keep learning from you and get started."

"I'm happy to hear that. I only mentor a few people at a time, but I can see that you're excited. Your background in nursing tells me you're a hard worker."

"I am, and I promise if you mentor me, I won't waste your time."

"I hold group meetings. It'll be you and two others. We meet at my home. Are you okay with that?"

"Absolutely. Don't worry about my job. I'll find ways to cover a shift if I need to."

"We're actually meeting this afternoon from four to five. You're welcome to join this meeting or wait for the next one the following week. Either way is fine with me."

"Brilliant. I have a holiday today. I'll be there at four sharp. Whereabouts are you?"

"I'm living in Maida Vale. Are you familiar with it?"

"Yes, of course. I have a car, so getting there won't be a problem."

Eddie's face tightened as he drew a breath. "Parking is terrible in my neighborhood. I highly advise you to take the Tube. I'm only a ten-minute walk from Warwick station. When you're on your way, message me, and I'll meet you there. It's a little tricky getting to my place."

"You don't need to do that. I can manage."

"I don't mind. I do this with everyone the first time they come over. After that, I'll let you manage on your own for the follow up meetings. Deal?" Eddie extended his arm.

Evie shook his hand. "Deal. Is there anything I need to do to prepare?"

"Dress comfortably and keep an open mind."

29

When Gray arrived at the station, neither Gaston nor Pratt was there. He glanced at his watch: eight a.m. *Hmm, casual start here.*

Gray headed back downstairs and picked up a coffee from a kiosk. Just as he was about to head back upstairs, his phone chimed. It was a text message from Green wanting to know when he was coming back. No *Hello, how are things?* No *I'm sorry I didn't answer your other messages.* No *Don't ever contact me again.* All she wanted to know was when he was coming back.

To be honest, Gray would have preferred one of the other messages. Because trying to answer her question was impossible. He didn't know when he was coming back. And telling her that was a no-go. Telling her maybe in a week would be even worse because she would hold him to it.

Gray took a few moments to strategize his response. But then it dawned on him that he had almost made a move on Pratt after dinner. Forget about the fact that she had a wife and he absolutely had no chance, but if he had, what was that saying about his and Green's relationship? As much as he liked her and wanted it to work out, the cold hard truth was that it wouldn't. His work schedule would always be a divider. What Green wanted from the relationship, Gray couldn't give. Unless he took up another career, he had zero wiggle room. So he answered her honestly: *I'm not sure. It could be a week. Could be more.* And he left it at that.

"Sterling!"

Gray looked up and saw Gaston walking toward him. He was dressed in old jeans and a black parka that was a size too big for him.

"You're an early bird," he said before taking a sip from a coffee cup.

"Old habit. I'm glad you're here. I'd love to share with you where I'm at with the profile."

"Brilliant. Can't wait to hear what you have."

Once they reached Gaston's desk, he wasted no time urging Gray to share his findings.

"Let's go," he said as he slipped off his parka and took a seat.

Gray picked up a pen and was getting ready to write down bullet points on pieces of paper when Gaston stopped him.

"We can put stuff up on the board later. Tell me what you have." He rested his forearms on the top of his thighs and eyed Gray.

"Okay. White male between the age of twenty-two and thirty. He's either self-employed or unemployed."

Gaston held up his hand and stopped Gray. "Sorry, I don't mean to be rude. I know all this demographic stuff about our killer. What I want is the meat. The one or two things that define this bastard."

Gray liked Gaston's directness. He liked that he wasn't screwing around and was dead serious about his investigation. Gray told Gaston about his observation of the victim's injuries and how he tied them into MMA classes at the gym.

"Brilliant," Gaston said, a large grin appearing on his face. "That's what I'm talking about. So the instructor is a person of interest. That's something I can dig into."

"I think you need to, but I don't think it's an instructor. My gut tells me it's another member because neither of our two victims at the gym took those classes, at least according to the manager. Also, it's too difficult to abduct someone from the gym, but I could be wrong. He might have hit it off with the women and went out for drinks, which is why I think it's worth exploring."

"So what are you proposing?"

"I believe our killer did source his victims from the gym, but they connected elsewhere. I think he's an MMA enthusiast who took classes there. So we need to look at men who were in those classes."

"Okay. I see your point. So he asked if they fancy a drink with him?"

"It's possible. It really could be anything to get them to agree to meet somewhere."

"Got it. I'll head back to the gym and see if I can question the instructor who teaches those classes. You're welcome to come along, if you want."

"Sure."

"How was your meal at the Black Forest?" Gaston asked.

Gray was about to answer that it was fine when a thought popped into his head. Pratt had said that she'd worked with Gaston on other investigations. Perhaps they were friends, and she'd already given him the lowdown of the dinner. Then Gray realized he was seriously overthinking it.

"It was great. The venison was delicious. How did your daughter do in her play?" he asked, not wanting to give any more details about dinner in case Gaston and Pratt did talk.

"Brilliant. She's a natural talent."

"I'm glad to hear that. She'll be the next Emma Watson sooner than later."

"If you're okay, we can pop over to the gym now."

Instead of taking the thirty-minute walk, Gaston hailed a cab, stating it would be the quickest way.

There was a different manager on duty that morning, but after a brief introduction and a bit of the same conversation they'd had with the previous manager, they were able to get the information they needed. Only it wasn't what they expected.

"Mia Thomas?" Gaston said. "It's a woman?"

"She's brilliant, and her class is always fully reserved well in advance," the manager said with a cheery smile.

"Is she the only instructor teaching these MMA classes?" Gaston asked.

"At the moment, yes."

"So you've had other instructors, then?"

"No. The MMA classes are new. We're always trying different things to keep our members motivated."

"I understand. And you have a record of all the people who have registered for the classes?"

"Members need to reserve a spot in each class through our app. So there's probably some way for that information to be pulled. I'll need to speak to our IT guy."

"If you could do that right now, that would be aces."

"Excuse me." The manager headed back to his office.

Gaston held up a piece of paper with the schedule for the MMA classes printed on it. Thomas didn't teach a class until later that evening. Gaston went ahead and called the number listed for her and asked if she was available for a short conversation.

"She's willing to meet. We can head over to her office after we're finished here," Gaston told Sterling. "Now, if the IT department can provide a list of men who have taken the MMA classes, we'll have a good start. Besides the security camera at reception, I didn't notice any others throughout the gym."

Gray was looking at the directory for the gym that hung on a wall. "Let's take a look at the room where the classes are taught. It's up on the third floor."

The two made their way to the room where the MMA classes were held. A yoga class was currently taking place in the space. There wasn't anything special about the room. Inside there were ten members, including the instructor, but it looked like it could accommodate more, maybe twenty-five people. Certainly enough room to lay out a soft mat and run through grappling moves. The floor also had three other spaces reserved for classes. There were more stationary bikes and treadmills along the windows running at the front of the building, in addition to more exercise machines.

Gray walked over to the windows and looked down at the street below. The foot traffic was just as heavy as it had been during their first visit. *He's definitely not taking them from here. He's got to be convincing them to voluntarily leave with him or meet him elsewhere.*

"Any thoughts so far?" Gaston said as he joined Gray at the window.

"One. Let's head back downstairs. I want to check something out."

Near the reception area was a large bulletin board where the gym posted information. There were a few advertisements for protein shakes and exercise clothing. But one flyer caught Gray's eye.

"This," he said, pointing to a small flyer.

"'Learn to trade cryptocurrencies,'" Gaston read out loud. "You looking for a career change?"

"No, but I think there are people here who might be, and this is the perfect method to lure someone to meet you, especially if you've had your eye on them."

30

Mia Thomas was willing to meet and answer questions if Gaston and Gray could come to her place of work. She was employed at one of the large consulting firms in the city and felt she could break away for a few minutes.

"Accountant by day, MMA fighter by night," Gaston said as he and Gray waited in the lobby of Thomas's office building.

A few moments later, an energetic woman with brown hair approached them.

"Hello," she said. "I'm Mia Thomas. You provided an excellent description. I spotted you as soon as I walked out of the elevator."

"I'm DI Gaston, and this is Special Agent Gray. Thank you for meeting us. This shouldn't take long. It's our understanding you're the only MMA instructor at Fitness World?"

"That's right. I was looking for a way to make extra money, and plus, I enjoy teaching. Is this about the classes I teach? Am I doing something wrong?"

"No, it's nothing like that. We're interested in members that attend your classes, in particular, the men. How familiar are you with them?"

Thomas shrugged. "About as familiar as an instructor can be teaching three classes a week. I don't associate with them outside of the gym, if that's what you're asking."

"Is it the same men in each class?"

"Usually. The class is always fully booked as soon as the reservations slots open up."

"Do you know their names?"

She shook her head. "Sorry. I only know them by their faces."

"But there are definitely a few who have attended all of your classes."

"Most of them have attended all the classes."

"I see. Any of those members stand out to you? Maybe something about their demeanor?"

She shrugged again. "I try to keep it professional, so I'm not really analyzing them."

"Mia, have any of these men come across as having prior MMA training?" Gray asked.

"There is one man who picked up on the moves fairly quickly. He was very enthusiastic, almost aggressive at times with the moves."

"So you think he might have had previous training?"

"The classes, even the advanced one I teach, are quite basic. I don't see how someone who has had any serious training could be interested. But like I said earlier. I'm not analyzing them."

"Can you recall this person's name?" Gaston asked.

"I don't think so."

The manager at the gym was able to provide a list of men who had taken the classes, along with their contact information. Gaston removed the list from a manila envelope.

"Can you tell me if any of these names sound familiar?"

Thomas looked over the names. "No. None of them ring a bell. Sorry."

"The aggressive member, the one who might have had prior training, could you describe him?"

"White skin, short brown hair, fit."

"Any distinguishing marks, like a mustache or a tattoo?"

"He was always clean-shaven. I didn't notice any tattoos. He just kind of looked very ordinary. Someone you wouldn't give a passing glance at."

"Was he tall? Short? Broad shoulders?"

"Taller than you," Thomas said, pointing to Gaston, "but not as tall as you." She pointed at Gray. "If I had to say something about his physique, I would say it leaned toward athletic. Sorry. I know I just described probably most of the men that go to a gym."

"You've done great," Gaston said. "We appreciate your time."

They bade goodbye to Thomas and headed out of the building.

"We should pull footage from the security camera on the nights that she teaches class," Gray said.

"I was thinking the same thing. We're looking for an ordinary joe."

Eddie got to the Tube station early. He wanted to be sure Evie did not walk off in search of his place. During the day, she had messaged twice asking for directions, insisting that she could find the place on her own. He finally relented and gave her an address. Still, he told her he would meet her at the entrance to the Tube station.

He waited across the road, near a tree and out of immediate sight. He wasn't sure if Evie would arrive alone, as directed, or with a friend who would wait at a nearby coffee shop. If someone did tag along, then the deal was off. Eddie would delete her contact information, forget all about her, and move on. Disobedience would not be tolerated one bit. There's a reason why the chain of command works. It's why the world is filled with alphas and betas. People must accept their place in society and play their roles. Of course, Eddie was a leader, a professional who knew best. Because of this, it was his responsibility to keep order, to ensure that others remained productive members of society. If Evie could demonstrate that, she'd walk away today.

Eddie spotted Evie right away. Arriving alone was her first test. She looked around as she remained at the Tube entrance. *So far, so good.*

"Evie!" Eddie called out as he crossed the road.

"Hi, Eddie."

"Did you have trouble getting here?"

"Not at all."

"Where are the others?" Evie asked as she kept in step.

"Poppy and Amy are on the way. They should be arriving soon. I've been mentoring those two for a month. We should hurry; I don't want to keep them waiting if they already arrived. Tom is another person who I've been mentoring for a while. He messaged me that he wouldn't be attending today."

"Is that a problem?"

"It would be if we had just started, but I've mentored him on and off for a year. Really, he doesn't need my help, but he usually tries to stop by when time permits."

"Is he doing well?"

"He's already resigned from his job and making more now than he ever had before."

"Brilliant."

"I'm just over there." Eddie pointed at a white row house with green trim.

Evie took her phone out and snapped a picture of the home as they approached.

"What was that for?" Eddie asked.

"My wife. In case she asks where I've been."

"Ah, I see. Did you not tell her you were coming here today?"

Evie shook her head. "I want to surprise her. Also, I want to learn a bit more so I can explain it to her correctly. She doesn't know much about cryptocurrency trading, and she'll have a bunch of questions. She's the curious type."

"I understand." *But taking a picture without asking permission is a strike against you.*

Eddie watched to see if she would send the photo straight away. She didn't, and there was hope he could salvage their meeting. Just then, Evie's phone rang.

"Hi, Lillie. Oh, nothing much, just out and about. How is everything at the office? Yes, of course. We can grab tea right after. Right. See you then."

"Your wife?"

"I need to pick her up after she finishes at work."

Eddie produced a key and unlocked the front door to his place.

"Please." Eddie allowed Evie to enter first. "I conduct the classes in the basement."

Eddie saw Evie tapping out a message. "So you changed your mind? Sending her the picture anyway?"

"Yeah, she's a worrywart."

"It's a shame."

"What is?" Evie asked as she looked up from her phone, puzzled.

"That you didn't ask my permission to send off a photo of my home."

"Oh, I didn't think it would be a problem. It's just a photo."

"Insubordination. That's your second strike."

Eddie struck quickly with a palm strike, snapping Evie's head back. She dropped to the floor, unconscious.

"There's a change to the lesson plan, Evie. And you're not going to like it."

31

When Gaston and Gray returned to the office, Pratt sat at an empty desk, tapping away on her laptop.

"Did the gym visit lead to anything new?" she asked with a smile.

"We have leads, but there'll be a bunch of information to sort through," Gaston said before briefing Pratt on what they'd learned.

"Well, we can rule out women, then blond men, and then men who don't fit the body type. That'll at least cut it down. It still sounds like a solid direction. If I can help with sorting through the footage, please let me know."

"There's a lot, so it's appreciated. The three of us can split the footage."

"When we narrow it down to men that fit Mia's description, we might get lucky and have someone jump out at us," Gray said. "At that point, staff should be able to identify any person of interest. Also, we can have Mia take a look at the culled list and see if she can ID her aggressive student."

They sorted through the footage for the rest of the afternoon, quickly eliminating anyone who didn't fit the description. They then made notes on the remaining men: the number of times they showed up at the gym during the hours when the class was held. In the end, they ended up with fifty-six men.

"It just dawned on me, there could be men who arrived much earlier to work out before the class," Pratt said.

"You're right," Gaston said, "but we have to start someplace. Hopefully, our aggressive student is one of these individuals."

Between the three of them, they identified twelve individuals they thought really fit Thomas's description and visited the gym almost every night she held a class. Gaston printed out screenshots of the men and tacked them to the board.

"Anyone has a favorite?" Gaston asked. "I know I have two."

He walked up and put a sticky note on the two that caught his eye.

Gray also had two picks, and one of them matched Gaston's pick. He put a sticky note on them. Pratt only had one pick, and it was also one of the two that Gaston had picked, but not the same as Gray's pick.

"Lillie, care to explain why you're preventing us from saying 'bull's-eye'?," Gray said with a smile.

"I like the guy you two picked. If I had to pick two, he would have been my other pick. I like this only because he seemed jittery during a few of his visits."

Both Gaston and Gray noted that was the exact reason why they had singled him out as well.

"So you two care to explain why you picked the other person?" Pratt asked.

"For me, it's his eyes," Gaston said. "They look dead. Sterling?"

"The same. No emotion."

"I'll message Mia these screenshots and see if any of these men is her aggressive student," Gaston said. "If she IDs one, we just need the staff to identify him, and we can pay him a visit."

"And if it's not?" Pratt asked.

"Then we'll need to consider all of these men," Gaston said.

Pratt looked at her watch. "I need to leave a little early. Do you mind?"

"Not at all," Gaston said.

"Evie picking you up?" Gray asked. He just realized an entire day had passed, and not once did he sense any awkwardness between Lillie and him. Maybe he was overthinking the whole thing.

"She is. Trying to get more of that quality time again."

"Great. Anything exciting planned?"

"Tea, possibly a quick bite to eat, but that's about it. She's usually so stressed at her job that she often just wants to relax at home. I don't mind."

"Enjoy yourselves."

"Cheers," Pratt said before grabbing her belongings and leaving.

"Have you met Evie?" Gray asked Gaston after Pratt had left.

"Yeah, she's great. Wonderful woman."

"She seems like it. I met her briefly last night after dinner. Do you need to cut out early? Feel free if you have obligations."

"I'm fine, mate."

Gaston and Gray spent the next thirty minutes talking about old cases while waiting for Thomas to respond.

"It's Mia," Gaston said as he picked up his ringing phone. "DI Gaston. Hi, Mia. Yes, I appreciate the call. Yes . . . Yes . . . I see. Are you positive? Brilliant. I appreciate your help with this. Thank you."

"Well?" Gray asked as he arched an eyebrow.

Gaston stood and tapped his finger on the individual they had all singled out. "This is the aggressive student."

Gray came up behind Gaston for a closer look. "All right, Mr. Jittery. Let's find out why you're on edge."

Gaston printed out copies of the screen grabs of all twelve members. He tucked them inside of a manila folder before he and Gary headed downstairs. As they exited the building, they noticed Pratt was still outside.

"Hey, you. Shouldn't you be long gone by now?" Gray asked.

"She's running late. At least, I think she is. She hasn't responded to any of my calls or messages."

"Is that like her?"

"Not at all. She normally responds right away when she's not on shift at the hospital. And even then, she's quick. I'm the slow one."

"Maybe she's caught up in traffic and doesn't want to text and drive," Gaston suggested.

"That's my thought," Pratt said. "The last message I got from her was earlier in the day, after a brief phone call. I thought maybe it was an accident because it made no sense."

"What was the message?" Gray asked.

"There was no message, just a photo." She showed the message to both Gray and Gaston.

"A picture of a house?" Gaston said. "Was she visiting a friend? Maybe she lost track of time and is still there."

"She said she was just out running errands. I thought it was weird when she sent it and intended to ask why, but I got sidetracked when my superior called. I forgot all about it until now."

"Do you want a lift?" Gaston asked. "I brought my car today. It's not a problem."

"I'm fine. Where were you two heading?"

"Good news. We heard back from Mia. The jittery guy is her aggressive student. We're on our way to the gym to see if someone there can ID him."

"That's wonderful news."

"Are you sure you're okay here?" Gaston asked.

"I'm fine. Go on."

"We'll be in touch if anything comes of it. Cheers."

32

After moving Evie to the cage in the basement, Eddie fixed himself a meal: two pan-fried chicken breasts seasoned with salt and pepper, steamed broccoli, and dry baked potato. While he ate, he deliberated on whether to attend class at the gym that night. Because of his meetings with Evie, he hadn't planned on it. But things had worked out in a way that had him reconsidering.

If Evie had done well, Eddie would have conducted the class and helped her further understand cryptocurrency trading. He would have made an excuse for Poppy and Amy not showing up. Evie would have learned something and been on her way. But it never worked out like that. Every person he'd brought back had failed to realize their position in life, and thus the lesson he was prepared to teach had to be changed.

Eddie had real hope for Evie. She seemed the responsible type, unlike the other girls who were from the gym. Evie wasn't a member of the gym. She'd heard about Eddie's class from a posting he'd left in a coffee shop near the gym. He'd started leaving his advertisement elsewhere, realizing he didn't need to watch the women beforehand. A neutral meeting in a pub or a coffee shop was enough for him to decide if they were worthy of being invited back to his place. Evie had been. Plus, he wanted to try a different breed of woman, someone who wasn't a gym rat.

It's decided. I'll take the class tonight. I have enough time to make it to the gym.

Eddie finished up his meal and then went upstairs to prepare. He stared into the bathroom mirror and applied a prosthetic nose, using liberal amounts of adhesive to keep it securely in place. He then applied fake muttonchops to the side of his face. He was always amazed at how adding those two things drastically changed his look. Lastly, he put in colored contact lenses, making his brown eyes green. He always wore a ball cap to gym, even in the classes. He'd watched his fair share of crime dramas. He knew enough to disguise himself, unlike other killers. *No matter how big the hammer is, you can't pound common sense into stupid people.*

When Evie woke, she knew immediately she was in a terrible situation. And it wasn't because she awoke in a dark room lying on the floor inside of a cage. She remembered being hit. She'd seen his hand coming straight at her face. That was the moment she realized her mistake.

Evie couldn't believe she had put herself in a position to have something like that happen to her. There was no shortage of times when her wife, Lillie, talked to her about being vigilant about her surroundings and who she was with. She knew she shouldn't have agreed to meet Eddie in his home after one meeting, or ever. She'd heard the horror stories from Lillie how most killers are not what one would suspect. Not once did Evie get an evil killer vibe during her meeting with Eddie. She had at least had the mind to snap a photo of Eddie's house. But what good had that done?

I'm so stupid. I'm married to an investigator with Interpol. Lillie has told me more stories than I can count of how easy it is for a woman to be abducted. The stories always started with how a man tricked a woman into going with them. Those women would always say, "He was nice. He was polite. He didn't seem threatening." Never in a million years would I ever think I'd be one of those women. I'd always told Lillie I was too bright for that. Seriously, how could anyone be that gullible? And now here I am, locked up in a cage in a lunatic's basement.

But there was one thing Evie had going for her: Lillie had insisted Evie learn self-defense, and not just a beginner class to learn just the bare basics. Evie had to pass Lillie's test. She'd run Evie through countless scenarios until she was satisfied Evie could defend herself if push came to shove. And it had.

Okay, Evie. All isn't lost. You're still alive. That means there's a way out of this. Focus and remain calm. Eddie isn't a big guy. You know enough to evade his attempts to grab you, choke you, or pin you down. You are capable of striking and kicking. He caught you off guard earlier. That's all that happened. But the tables have turned. You have the advantage. He'll never suspect an attack from you. That's the path out of this alive. Remember that.

Eddie hadn't reserved a spot in the upcoming MMA class as he figured he wouldn't be able to attend. When he did check the app, all of the spots had been filled. He still wanted to go to the gym anyway. Sometimes members didn't show, and a place would open up. He just needed to wait outside the class right before it started. He got to the gym a little early, so he jumped on the treadmill for a warm-up run.

33

"Hey, you know, we might get lucky and spot our jittery guy tonight," Gaston said as he and Gray entered the gym. "Mia's teaching a beginner class in thirty minutes."

"That works," Gray said.

Gaston went through the formalities of introducing Gray and himself to the staff at the front desk.

"Do you know if this member is here today?" Gaston showed the young lady the photo of their jittery suspect.

"I haven't seen him, but Alisa might have. She's busy with a new member, but she'll be back shortly."

"Is it all right if we have a look around? We'll check back a little later."

"Sure."

Gaston and Gray made their way up to the third floor. Both were eager to see if their jittery suspect was waiting for the class to start. A few men were lingering around outside the empty room. Thomas hadn't shown up yet.

"Excuse me, could any of you tell me if this is where the MMA class is taught?" Gaston asked.

"Yeah, it should be starting shortly," one of the men said.

"Cheers, mate."

"None of them is our guy," Gray whispered. "We should clear each floor one by one."

They searched the entire third floor, including the bathrooms, and continued on the second and first floors.

"Unless we missed him, he's not here," Gray said.

They headed back to the reception desk and found a different lady there.

"Hi. Are you Alisa?" Gaston asked.

"Yes, that's me. How can I help you?"

"I'm DI Gaston, and this is my colleague Special Agent Gray. Could you tell us if you saw this member here today?" Gaston showed Alisa the screengrab.

"I haven't, but I know him. He comes often."

"Brilliant. Could you tell us his name?"

"Oh, that I don't know. Members swipe their key card over there to gain entrance. If I had his key card, I could swipe it here and retrieve his contact information. Only my manager has access to that information without a member's key card. It's the company's way to protect our members' privacy."

"Of course. Is your manager in?" Gaston pointed to the door behind her.

"He's in a meeting, but it shouldn't take long. They usually aren't more than ten minutes."

"I see. But you're positive you haven't seen this man enter the gym today? He usually takes Mia's MMA class, which is starting very soon."

"Positive. He might just be running late."

"You're probably right."

Gaston turned around to face Gray, but he was staring out the entrance of the gym.

"What is it?" Gaston asked. "You see our guy?"

"No, but I just bumped into a member, literally, as he was heading out in a hurry."

"Was he one of the men upstairs waiting for Mia's class?"

"I'm not sure. You have the photos on your phone, right?"

Gaston pulled up the twelve individuals they had initially singled out, and Gray took a look at them.

"This is him, the one in the ball cap. That must be why he looked familiar."

Gaston turned around to Alisa. "Excuse me, are you familiar with this member?"

"Yes, he's also here quite a bit. He takes Mia's classes. I saw him come in."

"I wonder why he just left. Her class is starting any minute."

"I'm not sure."

The other young lady Gaston spoke to appeared, along with a few of the men waiting for the MMA class. The guy who had answered their earlier question about the class was a part of the group.

"Excuse me, mate. What happened to the class?" Gaston asked him.

"The instructor had to cancel."

"I see. Sorry to hear about that."

Gaston turned to speak to Gray, but he wasn't around.

"Excuse me, Alisa, did you see where my colleague went?"

"He's right there," she pointed.

Gray had just come back into the building.

"Something come up?"

"That guy I bumped into. I know he's familiar because he's one of the twelve, but my gut is telling me that's not the reason why I did a double-take. It was something about his face. I can't quite place it."

"What? You want to question him?"

"I do. That's why I ran out after him, but he'd already disappeared."

"No worries. We'll get his contact information from the manager and then pay him a visit. Hold on. My phone's ringing. DI Gaston. Lillie, what's wrong? Are you serious? Yes, we're about done here. We'll come back. No, it's no problem at all." Gaston hung up. "That was Lillie. She's still waiting for Evie. She's really worried, says she can't get a hold of her."

Gaston handed Alisa his business card. "Tell your manager to call me. I need these members identified along with their contact information," he said as he gave her the manila folder. "It's crucial."

34

Pratt was on her phone outside of the Metropolitan Police headquarters when Gray and Gaston arrived.

"Lillie," Gray called out.

Pratt lowered her phone. "I still can't get a hold of her. Everything inside of me is shouting something's wrong."

"Okay, let's work through this," Gray said. "You last spoke with her on the phone earlier today, correct?"

"Yes. We made plans for her to pick me up. I had asked what she was doing, and she said she was just out and about."

"Exact words?"

"Yes."

"Okay, then you hung up and . . . ?"

"About five minutes later, she sent me a photograph of a house. There was no explanation."

"And you meant to ask why but then you got sidetrack and forgot, right?"

"Yes. Why did I let that slip by? I've never done that before." Pratt's face tightened out of frustration.

"Hey, you did nothing wrong. Don't beat yourself up," Gaston said.

"And the house in the photo doesn't look familiar?" Gray continued with his questioning.

"No. I must have looked at it about a million times. You both know what I'm thinking. You have to be thinking it too."

Gray and Gaston gave each other a look.

"That photograph was a call for help," Pratt said. "It's the only explanation I can think of, and don't tell me I'm jumping to conclusions."

"I won't. It makes complete sense," Gray said. "Sometimes, the photograph will have GPS coordinates in the metadata. Send it to me."

The three went back upstairs, and Gray transferred the photograph to his laptop. He right-clicked on the picture and brought up the information. *Ah, there we go. Those are the latitude and longitude coordinates. We just need to punch them into Google Maps.* A few seconds later, the map zeroed in on a location: Maida Vale.

"That's a neighborhood north of Hyde Park," Gaston said.

"Does she have friends there?" Gray asked

"None that I'm aware of," Pratt said.

"Only one way to find out," Gaston said as he held up his car keys.

After learning that the MMA class had been canceled, Eddie hurried back to his home. He was beyond irritated. He'd been looking forward to that workout, wanting to let loose aggression that had built up from his encounter with Evie. Instead, the trip to the gym had made it worse. He'd even started ripping off his disguise on the walk back home from the Tube station. The sting from the adhesive pulling out a few hairs from his natural sideburns felt good. It made him crave another type of workout.

Guess what, Evie? I'm not waiting until tomorrow to give you a lesson in grappling.

As soon as Eddie was back in his house, he started the protocol for his class. He locked the front and the rear doors of his home with dead bolts. He then locked every single window. Satisfied, he headed into his bedroom, where he would prepare himself.

The white tunic with matching pants was freshly washed and starched to the right amount of firmness that Eddie liked. He removed the black belt from his dresser drawer and proudly held it up in front of him.

I earned this.

But that was debatable. Beginner judo students are referred to as kyu, and the belts they wear start with light blue, followed by white, purple, and then brown. Only after mastering a certain amount of moves and competency in judo can a person move on to the level of dan and earn their first black belt.

Many years ago, Eddie had a falling-out with his sensei at the dojo where he trained. He believed Eddie wasn't mentally ready to become a dan because he didn't fully respect the art of judo. He felt Eddie had shown a lot of disrespect, especially to his opponents, often failing to bow after a victorious match and instead choosing to taunt. It got worse whenever Eddie lost a match. Respect is the heart of judo. For a student to not take it seriously could result in being expelled, which was precisely what had happened to Eddie at three different dojos. It was around that time that Eddie became disillusioned with the entire practice of judo, considering the formalities and etiquette of the sport a monumental waste of time. Neither was required in a street fight. That's when he switched to training in MMA. But Eddie soon had problems in that arena as well. It seems respect went a long way in that sport too.

I don't care what anyone says. I am what I believe I am: a badass grappler.

Eddie climbed into the pants and then slipped on the tunic, placing the left side over the right. He next took his belt and put the middle part of it across his belly button so that the two ends of the belt were equal in length. He wrapped the belt around his back, crossing the strands over each other before bringing them back toward the front and crossing them once more. He looped one end under the other, stuck the other end through it, and pulled it tight. This was the only formality that Eddie practiced before facing an opponent. Getting dressed.

This is how it should be done. This is how students should be taught. Protect yourselves at all times, bitches.

You're a beast. Eddie beat his chest twice while looking in the mirror. When he reached the basement. He kicked the door open and entered the room with his arms held up.

"Welcome to class!" he shouted, startling Evie, who was curled up on the floor inside of the cage.

Eddie walked over to the water cooler in the corner and poured himself a cup of water. He slurped it down, smacking his lips when he'd finished. "Damn tasty water."

"Why are you doing this, Eddie?" Evie cried out. "I don't understand."

"Ah, ah, ah. In my class, you will address me as Sensei. I won't respond to anything else. So obey, obey, obey."

Evie sat up. "Please just let me go. I've done nothing to you."

"On the contrary, you actually did. I believe I mentioned it upstairs before smacking your face. You don't recall? Okay, a little refresher: You took a picture of my home without my permission. And you were about to send the photo to someone without my permission. I couldn't let the insubordination continue. You understand now?"

Eddie interlocked his hands and pressed outward, cracking his knuckles. He tilted his head side to side before rotating it in a circle to loosen up his neck.

Evie hooked her fingers on the mesh cage. "What's going to happen, Sensei?"

"We have your first lesson." Eddie slipped on black latex gloves.

"All I wanted to learn was cryptocurrency trading. That's all."

"Sorry, darling. That class has been canceled. You're now enrolled in MMA."

"Please, Sensei. If you let me go, I promise not to tell anyone. I swear it."

"Enough! The class has started."

Eddie produced a key.

"Now, when I open the door, I want you to move to the center of the mat. Understood?"

"If I prove to be an excellent student, what will happen?"

Eddie cocked his head. "I'm not sure. I need to see how well you perform."

"Okay. I'll do my best."

Eddie unlocked and removed the padlock before opening the cage door. He held out his hand.

"Come on. Show me what you can do."

35

Gaston, Pratt, and Gray had piled into Gaston's car and begun driving to Maida Vale. Pratt had pushed to move quickly, fearing the worst for Evie.

"I just know something terrible has happened. I can feel it in my bones," she said from the back seat. "One minute, everything is fine. The next, it's balls-up."

"Lillie, I'm gutted to hear about Evie, but all this negative thinking isn't helping," Gaston said. "We're three capable investigators. There isn't anything we can't overcome if we work together."

"Chi's right, Lillie," Gray said. "We'll find Evie. Everything will work out."

But Gray could understand why Pratt was worried. There was a serial killer on the loose in London who broke his victims into pieces. Evie was missing. Not a pretty thought to have running through one's mind.

"Sorry, guys," Pratt said. "It's just that Evie and I have been together for a while. I thought I'd conveyed the dangers in this city and—oh, here I go again with the negative thoughts. I can't help but think that she somehow fell into our killer's hand."

Gray turned around in his seat so he could look at Pratt. "Lillie, this might be difficult to talk about, but we need to. Let's assume that's what happened here. We must try to determine what actions might have led to it. Was there anything out of the ordinary that she'd talked about or done in the last week or so?"

Pratt took a moment to consider Gray's question. "Off the top of my head, nothing stands out."

"Okay, maybe it's not something completely out of the norm. Was she recently excited about something or complaining about something more than usual?"

"Well, she has been really stressed at work lately, but she's always a little stressed after a shift at the hospital."

"Okay, let's stick with this. Did she mention anything that was the cause of that added stress?"

"Over supper the other day, she did mention that how much she loved nursing but wasn't sure if she had the temperament to continue doing the job long term."

"So possibly she was thinking about a career change, even something as simple as changing hospitals to someplace a bit less hectic."

Pratt nodded. "Yes, it's possible that might be the reason for that comment. But she didn't say it exactly."

"Or did she? She said she wasn't sure how much longer she could continue working at the hospital. She's already thinking of alternatives. She might not have mentioned what they were if she hadn't quite figured them out yet."

"She does love to surprise me with things once it's all worked out. I will admit that."

"That's got to be it," Gaston said.

"What else did she mention?" Gray asked. "Don't filter. Tell us everything, even if you can't see how it could be important. Let Chi and me decide that."

"She talked about how amazing it would be to be minted, having enough money to do whatever one wanted whenever one felt like it. We often played a game we called 'Off to Where?' Basically, either one of us would say that, and the other person would have to respond where they would go right at that second if they could go anywhere."

"Did you play that game last night?" Gray asked.

"No, we didn't, but Evie had always talked about how cool it must be to one of those people who can work anywhere."

"A digital nomad," Gray said.

"Yes, that's the phrase she mentioned."

"So maybe thinking how she can work from home or be her own boss is something she'd been considering."

"Makes sense," Pratt said. "Evie knows me well enough to know I always have a ton of questions whenever she suggests something. So much that she'd learn to think things through before bringing it up with me."

"This house. It might be her doing just that," Gaston said. "She's working something out. You said earlier she was 'out and about.' Sterling, what do you think?"

"Lillie, has Evie ever visited the gym that our victims were members at?"

"Not that I'm aware of. It's possible. She had complained about a bit of weight gain."

"It would be convenient, especially if she needed to meet up with you after you finished work," Gaston said.

"I suppose you're right."

"Does she ever have to wait for you?" Gray asked.

"Sometimes . . . What are you getting at, Sterling?"

"Does she have a favorite place to wait?"

"There's a coffee shop about a fifteen-minute walk from the Met head-quarters that she likes."

Gray pulled out his phone and swiped through the recent photos he'd taken. "This is what I'm getting at." He showed Pratt the photograph.

"'Cryptocurrency trading. Work from home. Easy money,'" Pratt read.

"I remember that advertisement. It was posted in the gym," Gaston said.

"That's right," Gray said. "Evie might have seen this and called the number. I'm calling it right now." Gray dialed the number. "No one's picking up."

"Do you really think that's what happened?" Pratt asked.

"I'm thinking that our guy does go to the gym but can't abduct anyone from there. He needs them to come to him. This is the perfect way to do just that."

Gaston batted the steering wheel with his palm. "Bloody hell. He might have been chatting up our victims and suggesting the cryptocurrency idea."

"Exactly. They call, he arranges a meet, and it's done."

36

"Exit the cage," Eddie said.

Evie had heard all about the investigation Lillie had been working on and been privy to the horrific details. There was absolutely no doubt in her mind: Eddie was the man Lillie was hunting.

"I'm asking nicely," Eddie said.

This is your chance. Lillie trained you. You know what to do. And you have the advantage. He won't be expecting an attack.

"Okay. I'm ready for my lesson," Evie said, adding a bit more shakiness to her voice.

She grabbed hold of Eddie's hand and made her way out of the cage, using the forward momentum to follow through with a palm strike straight into Eddie's nose, causing him to stumble back in a daze.

Evie followed with a hard kick to his groin. Eddie let out a yell as he grabbed himself with both hands and dropped to his knees. Evie snatched him by his hair and pulled his face straight into a knee strike. Only then did she run.

Up the stairs she went, drawing deep breaths along the way. She burst through the door at the top and ran into the kitchen. All of the lights inside Eddie's home were off, leaving the place dark. Moonlight shone through the window over the sink. Evie quickly scanned the countertop for a knife holder but didn't see one.

Arm yourself. Evie yanked open the drawers and cupboards for a knife or anything sharp or capable of stabbing.

"You bitch!" Eddie called out from the basement.

She heard his stomping footsteps making their way up the stairs.

Evie yanked out drawer after drawer searching for a knife. *Where are they?*

Eddie was nearing the top of the stairs.

Get out of the house, Evie. Now!

She ran through a cased opening at the other end of the narrow kitchen and into a dining room. She moved quickly around the dining room table and through another doorway into a sitting room at the home's front.

There's the front door.

Evie ran straight to it, turned the knob, and pulled. But the door wouldn't budge. She yanked harder. It still wouldn't move. Then she noticed the dead bolt. *Shit!*

She tried the window to the left of the door. It also had a keyed lock on it. So did the window she tried after that.

"Evie!" Eddie called out. "You stupid bitch."

She spun around. Eddie stood hunched at the end of a narrow hallway. The light from the basement stairs lit up one side of his body. Blood was smeared across his face as he breathed in and out through his mouth. He started walking toward her, picking up speed with each step.

"You can't escape."

Evie darted to the right and up the stairs to the second floor. She could hear Eddie's booming footsteps pounding against the wooden floorboards. The first door she tried was locked. There was a bathroom, but for some reason, it didn't have a door. She ran down the hall to the master bedroom, slammed the door behind her, and locked it. She ran to a window that overlooked the road in front of the home.

There was a small eave just below the window. She remembered seeing it over the front door. If she could get out, she could jump down from there. Evie tried to lift up the double-hung window, but it wouldn't open.

"Help!" she screamed as she struggled to get the window open.

A loud bang against the bedroom door startled Evie. Eddie was trying to kick the door down.

Evie scanned the bedroom for something heavy to smash the glass. It was the only way she would get through that window. She grabbed a bottle of cologne off the dresser, but it was too small. She picked up a digital clock, but it felt cheap, like it would shatter to pieces instead of the glass.

Come on. There has to be something here.

The door cracked. Eddie was breaking through. Another kick followed by another loud crack. This time the door splintered down the middle. Evie saw Eddie peering through the crack.

"I see you!" he said in a menacing voice.

Evie ran into the master bedroom's bath. She picked up a shampoo bottle and ran back to the window. Just as she was about to strike the window, her eye caught sight of the lamp on the bedside table. The base was metal. She picked it up and felt it had significant weight. Evie yanked the cord out of the wall socket and slammed the bottom of the lamp into the window. But by then, Eddie had reached through the splintered opening and was searching for the doorknob.

37

Gaston drove slowly down the road. "Sterling, are you sure this is the location?"

"The home should be somewhere around here," Gray said. He looked up from the map on his phone and out his window. "It's one of these rowhouses."

"They all look the same," Gaston said. "I think it'll be easier if we get out and walk."

The three climbed out of the vehicle and looked up and down the street. They were near the middle of the block.

"Should we double back and walk the block again," Gaston said, "Or just keep going and then come back if we need to?"

"Well, we're almost at the halfway point," Gray said. "Why don't we just keep moving forward and then double back if we need to?"

Gaston and Pratt nodded in agreement, and the three started walking down the street, comparing houses to the photo Evie had sent.

"It's white with either a green or brown trim," Pratt said. "I can't really tell with the photo she sent. It's slightly blurry."

"It doesn't help that the streetlamps are low wattage and spread out," Gaston said.

"Quiet neighborhood," Gray said. "Not a lot of foot traffic."

"Wait, is this it?" Pratt stopped and held up her phone in front of a house.

"Kind of looks like it," Gaston said.

"Lights are off. Doesn't look like anyone is home. But let's find out for sure."

Gray led the way to the front door and knocked. Gaston took an opportunity to look into the house through a window.

"See anything?" Gray asked.

"Nothing."

Gray peeked through another window. "Yeah, I don't see any sign of life. What's usually behind these rowhouses? An alleyway?"

"Usually," Gaston answered.

Gray took a few steps back to get a better look at the house. He then compared it to the photo. "The color looks right, but this isn't it. Look at the windows on the second floor. They don't match the ones in the photo."

"You're right," Pratt said. "Sorry."

"Help!" a woman screamed in the distance.

All three of them turned on their heels, searching for the source.

"Help me!"

"That's Evie!" Pratt said.

"It's coming from down the street," Gaston shouted as he took off.

Evie called out once more, coupled with the sound of breaking glass.

"There!" Pratt pointed to the house across the street.

They could see a woman climbing out of a window on the second floor.

"Evie!" Pratt called out.

"Lillie, help me. He's trying to kill me!"

Evie made her way out of the building and had begun to hang over the side of the eave.

"Wait, Evie. Don't jump!" Pratt called out as she crossed over the side of the road. Gaston was right behind her.

"I can't. He wants to kill me!" Evie called out once more as she lowered herself until she hung off the side of the eave. She let go just as Gaston got beneath her, breaking her fall to the sidewalk.

Gray stopped on the other side of the road, across from the house. He hadn't run to help Evie as something else had caught his eye. Seeing Evie climb out of the window to escape the house triggered a flashback to Sara Luna, the surviving victim from the Iowa killings, as she ran out of Bowen's house. Gray blinked and shook his head. *It can't be. It's my mind playing tricks on me.*

Gray focused once more. Standing in the window that Evie had just climbed out was a man looking straight at Gray. He rubbed his eyes and then looked at the window once more. The man he'd seen standing there had disappeared.

"Sterling!" Gaston shouted, pulling Gray out of his temporary mind paralysis. "He's still inside the house," Gaston said.

Gray crossed the road and ran straight to the front door, kicking it as hard as he could. A loud cracking noise rang out. He kicked it once more and the door splintered alongside the doorknob. Gray drew a deep breath and kicked as hard as he could. This time the door flew open, and he ran inside, followed by Gaston.

"I saw him in the window," Gray said. "He's upstairs."

Gaston grabbed hold of Gray's arm. "Slow. We don't know if he's armed."

Neither Gray nor Gaston had a firearm.

Gray led the way up the stairs, listening for movement. When he reached the landing at the top, he flipped a light switch, and the hallway lit up.

He peeked down the hall toward the room where he'd seen the man. The door was broken down, and the room was dark.

"No place to run, pal. Come out." Gray said. "Don't make this any harder on yourself."

Gaston removed a small flashlight on his belt and aimed it into the room as the two men cautiously approached it.

"We're coming to you. Let's remain calm." Gaston said.

Step by step, they moved closer to the room, Gray moving with his back along the left wall, Gaston along the right wall. It was dead quiet.

When they reached the doorway, Gaston shone the light inside. From his angle, he saw nothing. He handed the flashlight to Gray, and he looked from his angle and saw nothing. He moved into the room, flipping on the light switch. Gray pointed at the bathroom door, which was closed. He pressed a finger against his lips and quietly went up to it and listened. Gray motioned to Gaston that on the count of three, he would open the door. He used his fingers and counted before pushing the door open. The bathroom was empty. They cleared the rest of the second floor and then the first, where they found the back door to the home ajar. He'd already escaped.

"We need to talk to Evie and get a description. He can't be far," Gaston said.

Back outside, Gray and Gaston found Pratt sitting next to Evie on the sidewalk, consoling her.

"How is she?" Gray asked.

"Aside from being shaken up, she's fine."

"Hi, Evie," Gray said as he knelt.

"Where is he?" she asked.

"He's gone, but it's important you give us a description so we can issue an APB. He can't be that far. But we need to act fast."

Evie's gaze fell to the sidewalk. "His name is Eddie."

Gaston made a note of the name.

"That's good," Gray said. "Does Eddie have a surname?"

"I don't know it. We never went beyond first names."

"Okay. Tell us everything you can about his appearance."

"He was white . . . had short brown hair and looked around twenty-five, I think. He had brown eyes."

"Any tattoos or earrings or facial hair?"

"No, none that I could see. He kept his face clean-shaven. He had some muscle on his frame. Definitely in great shape. Not as tall as you but taller than Chi."

"Did he speak with an accent; was he British or from somewhere else?"

"It was weird. At times he would speak with a slight British accent, and at other times he would sound American."

"He sounded like me?"

"Not quite. It was like a mixture."

Gray looked up at Gaston. "It's enough for an APB."

Gaston walked away as he made a call.

"You're doing fine, Evie. We need to hear everything while it's still fresh in your head."

Evie nodded.

"Did he say anything to you? Did you talk to him?"

"Yes, we talked. Did you see the classroom?"

"What classroom?"

"It's in the basement? The door is by the kitchen."

Gray popped up to his feet and ran back into the house, and found stairs. When he reached the bottom of the stairs, Gray felt like he'd been punched in the stomach. He stood there speechless.

"Sterling, what is it?" Gaston called out as he came down the stairs.

Gray didn't answer, so Gaston moved around him to have a better look at the basement.

"Bloody hell," Gaston said. "This must be a joke or something, right?"

"I have no idea," Gray said as he walked over to the cage. It was similar to the cage from his previous investigation.

"There's even a whiteboard hanging on the wall," Gaston said. "I've seen all the crime scene photos from your investigation. Either these are unbelievable coincidences, or your killer and my killer are somehow connected."

"It can't be," Gray said as he looked around the space, dumbfounded.

"Maybe it's a cult or something," Gaston said as he scratched the back of his head. You know, like some sort of teacher thing. Because this guy looks like he was conducting some type of class here. There's no desk in the cage, but everything else is similar. It was human biology, right? Your investigation?"

Gray nodded.

"But this looks like a gym class," Gaston said.

"Close, but I don't think he was teaching gym," Gray said. "Evie might be able to shed light on it, but I think he was teaching an MMA class. It explains all the broken bones and dislocated joints in your previous victims."

Gray and Gaston continued searching the home, spending extra time in the master bedroom.

"Hey, Sterling," Gaston called out from inside closet. "Looks like our guy was a fan of Jack the Ripper."

Gray walked over to the closet, where Gaston was down on his knees sorting through a pile of books.

Gaston held up a book. "He's got a collection of Ripper books."

"Let me see that." Gray took the book from Gaston and flipped through it. "You know the killer in Iowa also had a bunch of Jack the Ripper books."

"You think it means something?"

Gray shrugged. "They're certainly not the first to idolize the guy. Let me see that one, the one with the bookmark sticking out."

Gaston handed the book to him and Gray turned to the page that had been bookmarked. "I don't believe it."

"What? Did he mimic one of the kills?"

Gray showed him the bookmark. It was a piece of torn paper with a phrase written on it.

"'First one to five gets it all,'" Gaston read. "Does it mean something to you?"

"The killer in Iowa had the exact same quote in a picture frame."

38

The Metropolitan Police descended on Maida Vale in large numbers searching for Eddie. Still, as the hours wore on, the hope of catching him began to fade. And because the police were out canvassing the neighborhood, the media showed up. It didn't take long for the Jack the Ripper comparisons to start spreading on social media, even though the press had little knowledge of what had happened or that there was even a serial killer at large, or that there were books on the killer in the home. It also didn't help that anyone who had a phone had suddenly turned into a journalist and conducted live streams outside the house.

Pratt had taken Evie away before she could be identified as the victim by the media. Gray and Gaston could continue questioning her the following morning in the privacy of Pratt's home.

Gray helped with the search, thinking he would somehow pick Eddie out because he'd caught a glimpse of him in the window. Did he or had he imagined it? At the time, Gray questioned whether he'd seen him. *Of course I saw him. He was there. Even Evie confirmed he was there.*

When Evie described Eddie, she essentially described a typical athletic male with brown hair. She certainly didn't describe the jittery guy Gaston, Pratt, and Gray had singled out from the gym security footage. Had Gray gotten it all wrong? Was Eddie even at the gym?

Calm down, Sterling. Trust your gut. It has never let you down. Plus, the basement essentially makes your case. This is the guy.

But with that said, the classroom in the basement had him confused. He simply couldn't explain it. The cryptocurrency advertisement was also a strong lead he'd need to discuss with Evie. Surely, Pratt was also doing her own questioning. *Just be patient. It'll all come out.*

"Sterling!"

Gaston jogged over to him. "It's late. There's no need for us to stay here any longer."

"But . . ."

"Hey, I know exactly what you're thinking. The basement doesn't make sense to me either. But staying isn't helping matters. Let the bobbies do their job, and we'll do ours. We need to keep talking to Evie. Only then will we piece this together. Come on, I'll give you a lift back to your hotel. Get a good night's rest, and we'll take a fresh look at what we have in the morning."

Gray didn't bother arguing with Gaston. The two went back to his car and made the drive back into the city, both lost in their own thoughts.

"Sterling, I'll see you tomorrow morning," Gaston said as he pulled up to the Trafalgar.

"Bright and early, Chi," Gray said.

But Gray didn't believe for one second that he'd be able to sleep. He knew how his mind worked. He wouldn't stop thinking about what had transpired that night. That scene of Evie crawling off the eave and Eddie staring out the window at him played over and over. At least that's how his brain was relaying it. Gray couldn't even be sure if Eddie was looking at him or if he was confusing it with the flashback of Gary Bowen.

If only I had a better look at him. It might have made a difference. I would know if any of the men we singled out at the gym was Eddie or not. Gaston's voice popped into his head, reminding him that answers will come tomorrow. Gray knew all they needed to do was cross-reference Eddie's name with all members of the gym. It was an easy thing to check the list.

After a long hot shower, Gray crawled under the covers. He thought briefly about bullet pointing his thoughts on his laptop but decided against it. He needed to give his mind a rest. Sometimes getting away from a problem can help one see it differently, which can lead to alternate answers.

Gray drifted off to sleep a few minutes later, but it was anything but restful. He tossed and turned all night. It was the same dream over and over: Gary Bowen exiting his home, looking directly at Gray, and laughing before chasing after Sara Luna.

At some point, the dream transformed from Bowen laughing at him to Bowen taunting him. He would burst out the front door and shout, *You can't stop me, Sterling. It's impossible. I'll keep killing.*

Gray woke the following day with a pounding headache and feeling no more rested than when he'd gone to bed the night before.

When he arrived at headquarters, Gaston was already there, staring at the screenshots of the men they had singled out from the gym.

"Good morning, Chi," Gray said before taking a sip from a coffee cup.

"Hey, Sterling. I've made some headway, but it's not the news we want to hear. I was able to get in touch with a manager at the gym. They don't have a member named Eddie."

"Really? Eddie is a pretty common name. What about Edward?"

"I checked that name as well. Nothing."

"Have you heard from Lillie?"

"I have. She spent some time questioning Evie. She even showed her the men we have up here on the board." Gaston pointed to the screen grabs. "None of them look like Eddie. I'm still trying to find out if Eddie owns the home or is renting. We might be able to identify him that way."

Gray slowly shook his head. "This is not how I thought the day would start off."

"All is not lost. There is one bright spot. Lillie confirmed that the cryptocurrency advertisement is how Evie contacted Eddie. She said Evie thought Eddie seemed honest and genuine and that he was currently mentoring three others. When he suggested mentoring her, she jumped at that chance."

"He knew exactly what buttons to press to get her to say yes. He's not looking for people who are fitness fanatics. He's preying on people who want a better life. This totally tracks with what Lillie was saying about Evie wanting a change from her current profession."

"One other thing: Lillie said Evie saw the advertisement in a coffee shop near the gym."

"So he might have been posting these flyers all over the place."

Gaston nodded. "I told Lillie once you got here, we'd head over to her place."

"Sounds good."

"Sterling, have you had any additional thoughts on those coincidences?"

Gray drew a deep breath. "I've been tearing my hair out for an explanation. I haven't found one that works. Media coverage on my previous investigation was minimal. I don't see how he could have learned about what was happening in Ames, Iowa, and started copying. Both men started abducting people around the same time. Did Lillie say anything about the classroom?"

"She didn't. I'm not sure she even made the connection yet. If she saw the basement, perhaps she might have. What about the Ripper books?"

"I'm not all that concerned about them. A lot of people have a fascination with that man. Look at the stories the media is running now. For me it's the basement and that bookmark we found. It looks handwritten. We should see if the lab can confirm that it is and not just a print of something handwritten. I'll reach out to the investigators back in Ames and see if they can do the same. I know it was bagged."

"If it is handwritten, that would connect the two."

"I know. It's crazy."

39

Lillie and Evie lived in a flat on Tadema Road, located at the western end of Chelsea. There were no convenient Tube stops near their place, so Gaston drove. It only took twenty minutes to get there. Lillie met them at the front door, and she looked as if she hadn't slept a wink all night.

"Hi, Lillie," Gray said. "How are you two holding up?"

"As well as can be. I was finally able to get Evie to sleep around three in the morning, but she kept waking up from the nightmares."

"I can imagine." Gray briefly thought back to nightmares that interrupted his sleep.

"I was just making a kettle of tea. I'll bring you two a cuppa and then get Evie. She's upstairs."

Gray and Gaston sipped their tea while they waited in a small sitting room. A few minutes later, Pratt and Evie came down the stairs. Evie had her arms wrapped around her chest, hugging herself. She was dressed in an oversize T-shirt and leggings. Her eyes didn't look as tired as Pratt's, but Gray could tell she was still shaken by the ordeal.

Evie and Pratt sat on a sofa opposite Gray and Gaston. Evie kept looking away, unable to hold eye contact.

"Evie, I know talking to us right now won't be pleasant," Gaston said. "But it's important."

"It's fine. I want to do this."

"Okay. Could you walk us through the timeline of when you first contacted Eddie to when you ended up at his home and you knew something wasn't right?"

Evie nodded. "I saw his advertisement in a coffee shop, the one I always like to visit when I'm waiting for Lillie."

"It's near the gym, correct?" Gaston asked.

"That's right. Making a career change or trying something different was already top of my mind. I called the number, not really giving it much thought. The voice on the other end sounded pleasant. He briefly told me that we could meet in a public place, and he would give me a brief overview of how trading cryptocurrency works. There was no cost, no strings attached or anything like that, so I agreed to meet him at a coffee shop near our place."

Gaston readied his pen and notepad. "And what was the name of this coffee shop?"

"It's called Cuppa. It's right down the street from here, not far."

"Okay, you meet with Eddie, and the meeting goes well?"

"Yeah. I liked what he had to say. It sounded perfect. He gave me examples of other people he had taught and how they went on to be successful. I honestly didn't see any signs of him being what he was."

"Of course. So you scheduled another appointment?"

"Eddie said he holds weekly meetings at his home. He had one that same day in the afternoon at four, with all the people he mentors. It's a group thing. That's the only reason why I agreed to go there. He told me he would meet me at the Tube station and escort me. I thought it was strange and that I could find his place if he gave me the address, but he said everyone always has trouble finding it the first time. He would show me once, and then after, I could make my own way for future meetings."

"Perfectly reasonable explanation. What was he wearing? Do you remember?"

"He had a ball cap on. It was pulled low. A dark windbreaker and jeans."

Gaston took a moment to think. "Did the ball cap have a name or a logo stitched to the front?"

"No, it was just a plain navy blue cap."

"Okay, so you meet him at the Tube station, and you two walk directly back to his place?"

"Yes, but I'm still a little cautious, so when we get there, I take a picture of his home with my phone, just in case. He immediately asked why I did that. I told him so I wouldn't have trouble finding it the next time."

"But that's not the reason why you took it, right?" Gaston asked.

"No, I wanted to send it to Lillie just in case."

"Which you did a little later, but there was no message attached."

"Not quite. It was very quiet when we entered his home, and I didn't immediately see the others. He said two of them were already there, which was weird because he said they were on their way earlier. Right then, I decided to send a message to Lillie. I was just about to type out something when he hit me. I must have accidentally sent the message during that time because the next thing I knew, I woke up in a cage. The room was completely dark, so it took a minute for me to work out that I was in a basement. Once my eyes adjusted, I could make out other parts of the room. There was a small curtained window, but a little light got through the edges, which helped."

Gray moved closer to the edge of his seat. "So Eddie wasn't there when you woke?"

She shook her head. "I'm not sure how long I was alone, a couple of hours, maybe. My belongings were missing, so I didn't have my watch or phone. If I had to guess, I waited an hour or two at the most from when I woke until he appeared. He was clearly irritated. He was dressed in a martial arts outfit: white pants and top with a black belt."

Gaston scribbled in his notepad. "You two had a conversation at that point."

"I called him Eddie, and he said I had to call him Sensei. I was a student. He was very adamant about this. I pleaded with him to let me go, that I had done nothing to him, but he said I had done two things wrong. I had taken a photo of his home without his permission, and then I tried sending it to someone without his permission. He said it was insubordination. Once he said that, I knew discipline was the next thing coming."

"So you realized who he was at this point?"

"I assumed shortly after I woke. I'd heard enough about the investigation from Lillie that I guessed Eddie had to be the guy. After listening to him talk, I was convinced he was the killer. I figured I had one chance to surprise him."

"I'd taught Evie self-defense," Pratt said. "She's more than capable of defending herself."

"If it weren't for Lillie . . ." Evie's voice cracked, and her eyes began to well.

Pratt gave Evie's hand a comforting squeeze.

"Do you want to take a break, Evie?" Gaston asked.

"No," she said as she dabbed her eyes with a tissue. "When Eddie opened the cage, he held out his hand to help me out. I hit him as hard as I could right in his nose. I kicked him in the crotch and then slammed his face into my knee. I ran out of the room after that."

"Look at you." Gaston smiled. "You're a tough one."

A crooked smile formed on Evie's face. "The stairs led me up near the kitchen. I tried to find a knife for protection, but there were none. So I ran to the front door to get out, but the door had a dead bolt on it. I had no place to go but up the stairs to the second floor. Eddie had already come up from the basement. I locked myself in his bedroom and climbed out his window. That's when you three showed up."

"Two more questions," Gray said. "Did he ever mention or talk about Jack the Ripper?"

"No, not that I can recall. Why?"

"He had a collection of books on the guy in his closet."

"And the other question," Evie said as she caught Gray's eye.

"Does the phrase 'first one to five gets it all' mean anything? It's off a handwritten note that Eddie used as bookmark in one of the books."

"Sorry, that doesn't sound familiar either."

"I have something for you," Pratt said as she stood.

When she returned a few moments later, she handed Gaston a plastic bag.

"That's the shirt Evie was wearing. The blood splatter on it is from Eddie."

"Brilliant. I'll get this to the lab. We're one step closer to identifying Eddie."

"Do you think you'll catch him?" Evie asked.

"I promise we'll get him," Gaston said.

40

Gray and Gaston ended their conversation with Evie shortly after. Both were keen to head to the coffee shop where she had met Eddie, hoping there was security camera footage. According to Pratt, Cuppa was on Kings Road, only a fifteen-minute walk from her place.

The tiny bell on the shop door rang out as Gaston and Gray entered. The place was small, seating for no more than ten people spread out across five tables. The first thing Gray did was point out the camera aimed at the cash register. Sadly, it was the only one they saw. Gaston approached the girl behind the counter, made the introductions, and asked to speak to the manager or owner of the place. They stood away from the register as they waited. A few minutes later, a middle-aged woman approached them.

"Hello, I'm Maggie Smith, the owner. How can I help you?"

"I'm DI Gaston, and this is my colleague Special Agent Gray. This won't take up much of your time. We're working on an investigation and have a few questions."

"Sure. What would you like to know?"

"First, is that camera working?"

Smith looked over her shoulder to where Gaston had pointed. "Yes, of course."

"Do you have footage stored from yesterday, from six-thirty in the morning to eight?"

"Yes. Everything is backed up for forty-eight hours. If you want, you're welcome to come back to my office, and I can show you the footage right now. It won't take long to scroll through that time frame."

Gaston and Gray followed Smith through a door behind the counter.

"I'm assuming you're looking for someone," she said. "I'm here every day."

Gaston described the individual. "Does that person sound familiar?"

"It's a pretty generic description, but if he was wearing a ball cap, it'd be easy to find him in the footage."

Smith tapped on the keyboard to the computer sitting on her desk. After a few moments, a video of the shop's security footage began to play. She advanced the footage to the time Gaston had mentioned.

"Do you want to watch it in real time or skim until we see a man in a ball cap?"

"We're fine with skimming through it," Gaston said.

A man in a navy blue cap appeared at the counter a little before seven and ordered a drink, but the ball cap lid obscured his face. The angle of the camera looking down at him didn't help matters.

"Do you remember seeing this man?" Gaston asked.

"No, I don't. I might have stepped into my office for a moment. But I'm usually out front because of the morning rush. That's Julie helping him. Her shift doesn't start until the afternoon, if you want to speak with her."

Gaston nodded. "Let's keep looking."

Smith advanced the footage until Gaston stopped her.

"That's Evie walking past the counter."

"It is. Same clothes," Gray said as he leaned forward.

"Do you remember seeing this woman?" Gaston asked.

"Of course. I know Evie. She comes in here all the time. She bought a cookie on her way out. Did something happen to Evie?"

"Evie's fine."

They went through the remainder of the footage, and sure enough, the man with the ball cap was seen leaving first. Evie stopped at the counter to buy a cookie.

"That has to be him," Gaston said. "Ms. Smith, is it possible to give me this footage?"

"Sure, I can download the clip and email it to you."

Gaston handed Smith his business card. "My email address is on there. We appreciate your time."

"Rotten luck," Gaston said after they exited the shop. "We're quickly running out of ways to identify Eddie."

"Let's visit the coffee shop where Evie saw the flyer," Gray said. "Maybe we'll have better luck there."

They headed back to Gaston's car and made the drive. Once inside the coffee shop, the manager told them that permission wasn't needed to post information to the community board. In addition, the shop only stored the last seventy-two hours of footage. Gaston asked for it all to be emailed to him.

"I'm feeling less hopeful with this footage," Gaston said as they walked back to his car.

"We have his DNA on Evie's shirt. He might be in the system," Gray said. "Also, you're still waiting on the city records for ownership of the property. There's still hope."

Once at the station, Gaston handed Evie's shirt over to the lab and asked them to put a rush on it. Back at his desk, he got on the phone with city records while Gray started looking through the footage from the second coffee shop.

"They're still working on the property ownership request," Gaston said. "What date are you looking at?"

"I'm looking at the last twenty-four hours," Gray answered.

"I'll start looking at the twenty-four hours before that. Sterling, I want you to know I appreciate you helping out with the footage. I know it's a little out of your job description."

"My job is to help you catch this guy. Period."

41

Eddie had come up with a plan should things go wrong, which they had. He'd put together a go-bag and kept it in his closet. He'd learned about this helpful tool while watching spy shows on television. As soon as he saw those three individuals outside his home, he grabbed it and had ran out the back door. The bag contained clothes, a different nose prosthetic, colored contact lenses, and a fake goatee. He had slipped into a small area between two buildings and quickly changed out of his judogi. He'd then walked into the nearest pub, went straight to the bathroom, and put on the disguise. When he'd finished, he calmly exited the bathroom and ordered a pint. And that's how Eddie eluded the manhunt.

It had taken less than an hour for breaking news to interrupt the sporting event on the telly in the pub. The media reported that a woman had been held hostage in a home but escaped with the help of the Metropolitan Police.

No uniforms. They must have been undercover, he'd thought. *That's fine. So was I.*

Eddie wasn't quite sure how he felt about making the evening news that night. He'd never thought what he was doing would ever gain the attention of London, but when he had looked around the pub, everyone had been paying attention.

"What a bloody psycho!" a man had shouted. "Minging!" another person had said.

It had become clear what the general public thought of Eddie's actions.

Bloody fools. That's what they are. They'll never understand. This wasn't done for your approval or your entertainment. You're all just a bunch of brainless puppets. You do as you're told. I won't. Not me. My sensei wanted to say to me what I could be. Did I give him that power? No. And I've already achieved more than he thought I would. I've broken three women. Snapping them like twigs. Who in any dojo can claim that? None. So who is the failure? My sensei was afraid my talent would overshadow his skills. So he did the only thing he could do: suppress me. Joke's on you, Sensei.

That night, Eddie chuckled quietly to himself while he continued to drink his pint. He was about to leave when, on the telly, he caught sight of the two men he'd seen approach his home while Evie was escaping. They were standing behind the news reporter in the newscast. Eddie had remembered the tall, clean-cut one. He'd locked eyes with the man when he stood across the street. The shorter man had been concerned with Evie, but the tall one hadn't. *You were interested in me. Why was that?*

Eddie had started videoing the newscast with his phone until both men exited the frame. He'd then searched online for detective inspectors with the Metropolitan Police. The website didn't list their DIs, but a few LinkedIn profiles had come up in his search. The short man had one: DI Chi Gaston.

So you're a DI. Who's your partner?

Eddie had continued looking at the profiles on the professional networking site but hadn't been able to find one for the taller man. As he studied the man's face, his clothing, and his mannerisms, a thought had come to him. He looked American.

Now, what agency would send someone to help the Met? The CIA? The FBI? Interpol? He looks like a suit. Why would the FBI concern themselves with a murder investigation in London? Why the interest? Unless . . . wait, is that it? Are you a profiler? Are you like Clarice Starling from The Silence of the Lambs? *Is it your job to try to understand my motivation? So the Met brought you here to pass judgment on me, right? You're here to determine what kind of monster I am, right? You can't define me. I won't let you.*

That night at the pub, it didn't take Eddie very long to locate the agent's profile on LinkedIn once he knew what to look for. The mystery suit was Special Agent Sterling Gray of the esteemed Behavioral Analysis Unit. Eddie left the pub with just one thought on his mind: give Special Agent Gray a lesson in behavior.

42

It was late in the afternoon when Gray threw his hands up in the air. "I can't believe this."

"Believe what?" Gaston asked as he looked up from his laptop.

"Come over here and look at this."

Gaston rolled his chair over to where Gray was sitting and peered over his shoulder. "You found something?" he asked.

"I did. Look at the bulletin board. No flyer." Gray advanced the footage. "Now, here's the flyer."

"Who posted it?"

"That's the problem. A group of people, they look like tourists, walked into the shop. Our guy had to be mixed in with the crowd because before the crowd, no flyer. After the crowd, there's a flyer."

"Talk about rotten luck," Gaston said as he wheeled himself back to his desk. He picked up his phone and made a call. "It's DI Gaston. Anything on that DNA sample? You did? And? Are you sure? Run it through the database again and call me back."

"They get a hit?" Gray asked.

"The lab confirmed the blood is from a male person. But they came up empty when they ran it through our PNC. I told them to rerun it."

"We need Lillie to access Interpol's DNA database. We might as well do a global search just to rule it out."

"You're right. I'll have the lab send her the DNA profile."

"Include me in that email. I can speed things up by accessing the Bureau's NDIS database myself. Sooner or later, we'll catch a break."

Just then, Gaston's phone rang. "DI Gaston. Yes, I am. Just a minute." Gaston grabbed a pen and jotted a note down on a piece of paper. "Thank you. I appreciate it." Gaston hung up. "We got a name on the ownership of the home. It's not Eddie. The owner is Oliver Payne. I have a number." Gaston dialed the number. "Hello. This is DI Gaston with the Metropolitan Police. I'm looking for Mr. Oliver Payne. Oh, this is. If you have a moment, I'd like to ask you a few questions. Yes, this is about the house on Maida Vale. Yes, I'm sure you've seen the news coverage. Would you mind giving me the name of the tenant renting the house from you? What's that? Is he the only tenant listed on the lease? I see. Do you happen to have a contact number for him? That's the landline in the home. What about a cell number? Was there any other contact information? I understand. Do you have any copies of his identification? I see. Mr. Payne, if you think of anything else, please give me a call." Gaston ended the call after giving Payne his contact information.

"What did he say?" Gray asked.

"The name he has on the lease is Michael Baker. He doesn't have a cell number as he always calls him on the landline in the home, which Mr. Payne installed under his own name. It's included in the lease, which was verbal. Nothing in writing. Mr. Payne said Eddie always paid by money order, which he sent through the post. The name is probably fake."

"Let's run that name through every database we can access just to be sure," Gray said.

Gray had been hopeful when he arrived at the station earlier that morning. They had many leads to chase down, but so far, none of them had produced the information they needed: Eddie's full name or a photo of him. Gray had to consider that even the name Eddie might very well be fake. But Gray wasn't about to let any of that deter him. He had to believe somehow, one of those leads, when paired up with another in the right way, would lead to Eddie's true identity and, ultimately, his capture.

"He's on the run," Gaston said. "Do you think it makes sense to get an artist to do a sketch of Eddie based on Evie's description and give it to the media?"

"Tough call. He has the advantage. It might force him underground for good. Based on what I know now, I don't think he's a mission-oriented killer, there may be some sense of that, but I'm now convinced he's more of a control freak. That's what's really driving him. He feels the need to be one hundred percent in control of himself and how he appears to others."

"So breaking those women into pieces is his way of proving his worth?"

"In a contrived way, yes. He might have been ridiculed in the past or never shown the respect he believes he'd earned, and now he's trying to prove that he is capable."

"A bloody bastard with a grudge," Gaston said.

"That's another way to put it. The other potential outcome of making him famous is that it increases his drive. That could lead to more killings."

"Attack people out in the open? Random?"

"Possibly. But he's not stupid. He has thought this through enough to have a few failsafe plans in place. The fake names, no contracts, avoiding security cameras."

"He could also be disguised," Gaston said.

"The attention can force him to make mistakes, but it's not a gamble I'd like to wager right now."

"So what do you suggest we do?"

Gray leaned back in his chair. "We need to bait him. Give him a target, something he can focus on. Something that will convince him that it's the one thing he needs to do to redeem himself."

"We don't even know who this guy is. How are we drawing him out?"

"That's a good question."

"You should have the DNA profile in your mailbox," Gaston said.

Gray logged into the Bureau's secure server and accessed the NDIS database. He waited a few moments while the database did its thing. Gray yawned as he leaned back in his chair. He could feel the effects of his sleepless night taking hold of him. He wasn't sure how long he'd been in a daze, staring at the ceiling; probably no more than five minutes. But when he sat up and looked at his laptop, he nearly choked on his breath.

"Holy cow! I got a hit!"

"What?" Gaston popped off his chair.

Gray pulled up the file.

"Who's the guy?"

"Wait a minute. This can't be right." In an instant, his pumped-up chest deflated, and he sank back down into his chair.

"What?" Gaston said. "Spit it out."

"It has to be a mistake. A false positive." Gray looked up at Gaston. "The DNA is a match with Gary Bowen. The killer in Iowa."

"Hold on. Let's not kill the messenger just yet," Gaston said as he scratched his head. "Maybe they're distant cousins or something."

"Impossible."

"Why's that?"

"Because the match is one hundred percent. There's only one way two people can share DNA like that. They're identical twins."

43

Gray sat in his chair slack-jawed. He had run the search five more times, and each time, the NDIS returned the same results. Gaston sat opposite him with his face buried in his hands.

"I would have recognized a replica of Bowen if they were, in fact, identical twins," Gray said. "The individuals we singled out from the gym look nothing like Bowen. Eddie's footage in the coffee shop when he met with Evie didn't wave a red flag. I mean, physically, they're sort of the same, but..."

"Hey, we never ever got a good look at Eddie's face," Gaston said. "We were working off a description. How could either of us have known?"

The nightmares Gray had the night before had his mind twisted. He felt as if he were starring in his own psychological horror movie. Had he really gotten a good look at Eddie in that window? Did he immediately discount the similarities and convince himself it was his mind playing tricks by making him think it was a flashback?

"Did Bowen have any known family?" Gaston asked.

"As far as I understood, he didn't have any family. Actually, I take that back. The detectives I worked the case with never mentioned family or siblings. I just assumed he was all there was. Nothing prompted me to dig into his background ... until now."

"But they would have known, right, if he had an identical twin."

"I would think so. Both detectives have lived in Ames for quite some time and worked in law enforcement during that time as well. It's not that big of a town. I need to reach out to them and confirm this, because right now, it doesn't make any sense."

"We have a DNA match, but it could be wrong," Gaston said. "They could be a cousin, but even then, the odds of two people on opposite sides of the pond essentially murdering people in similar fashion are out of this world."

"I wonder if they were actually in communication. We need to scrub Eddie's home for anything that could connect him to Gary Bowen: a computer, email account, phone records, mail, anything. I need to know if what we have here is true."

"The CSI team might still be at the house."

"Let's take a ride there," Gray said as he stood. "I'd like a fresh look at the place."

Fifteen minutes later, Gaston and Gray were on the road heading to Eddie's home.

"It explains everything," Gray said as he stared out his window. "The cage. The classroom. The teacher-student relationship. The plastic bags . . . It's like one mind operating as two. It also explains the same fascination with Jack the Ripper and why they have the same quote."

"Twins often finish each other's sentences, and they're known to have the same thoughts," Gaston said. "But this, killing in the same way . . . It begs the question, was this planned or done independently?"

"Well, if it's a little brotherly competition, it explains why they possessed the same quote."

"First one to have five kills wins."

"Exactly. It doesn't matter now. We know who we're looking for." Gray removed his phone from his jacket and pulled up a photo of Gary Bowen. He showed it to Gaston. "Essentially, this is what Eddie looks like."

Gray texted the photograph to Pratt and asked her to show it to Evie. In the meantime, Gray made two calls: one to Detective Patton and the other to Detective Sparks with the Iowa Police. Neither man picked up, so he left messages asking for them to return his call.

A few minutes later, Gray's phone rang.

"Sterling here."

"It's Lillie. Why are you asking me to show a picture of Gary Bowen to Evie?"

"Just a minute, I'm putting you on speakerphone. I'm with Chi. Now to answer your question. According to the NDIS database, Eddie's DNA is a one hundred percent match with Gary Bowen. They're identical twins."

Pratt didn't say a word.

"Are you still there?" Gray asked as he glanced at Gaston.

"Yes, I'm sorry. I just needed a moment to grasp what you're saying."

"Chi and I were in the same spot a few minutes ago, but I ran the search six times. Same result each time."

"But how can this be?"

"We're not sure yet. But seeing if Evie recognizes Eddie is a good start to confirming if the DNA match is correct or not. I'll reach out to law enforcement back in Iowa and let them know what we discovered. Chi and I are on our way to Eddie's place to see if we can find any communication between the two . . . Yes, we'll hold."

A few moments later, Pratt came back on the line.

"I showed her the photo without saying anything. She ID'd Bowen as Eddie straight away. She said it was like seeing a mirror image. I still can't believe it."

"Neither can Chi and I. The odds are incredible."

"And you had no idea Bowen had a brother?"

"I didn't think he had any family. We'll know soon enough when I speak to the two detectives. But setting aside the *X-Files* aspect of all of this, we at least know who we're looking for, physically. As you can already surmise, none of the individuals at the gym match Bowen's description. Chi suggested he might be disguised. We should also assume Eddie isn't his real name. I'll keep you posted if anything comes from our visit to his house."

Gray ended the call. "We might need to have another conversation with Evie . . . See if he mentioned family or friends."

"You still think it's a bad idea to give that photo to the media?" Gaston asked.

"I would have initially said yes, but considering the tie-in to the Iowa murders, I don't know if it's our best play right now. We could have an advantage. We know Eddie is a twin, and we know what he looks like."

"You think he realizes that?"

"None of his actions suggest he does. Put out an APB, and we move ahead as if he doesn't and see if we can get the jump on him."

Eddie had been camped out across from the Metropolitan Police for quite some time. If his hunch was correct, Agent Gray would either be coming or going from there. And since Eddie believed it was Gray who had disrupted his plan, he had nothing better to do than to wait.

The hotshot agent has come to save the day. Bumbling bobbies needed help on a case. Was I really that good? Or are they really that lame? As much as I'd like to take credit for my ways, I do believe their stupidity didn't help matters. I had taken the precautions. I had come up with a contingency plan. I thought about what would happen when things went wrong. I shouldn't be in this predicament. Had my brother—my stupid little brother—listened to me and done as he was told, he wouldn't be dead.

When Eddie had discovered the police had killed his brother, he had simply shrugged it off.

That was his biggest problem: he never listened to me. Serves him right. But now he's made problems for me. I'm guessing Agent Gray helped out with my brother's investigation. Gary was sloppy. That was always his problem. And it didn't help matters when he blamed his failures on others. He probably made it really easy for Agent Gray to catch him. He probably even tipped off the agent somehow. It's the only way to explain why Gray's here in London. My brother, the screwup. Always leaving behind a mess I have to clean up. Fine by me. Agent Gray is just another piece of trash I can put in a bag and toss off to the side of the road.

Eddie was still wearing his disguise with his ball cap pulled low over his head. He was near Downing Street, blending in with the hordes of tourists in the area.

Come on, Agent Gray, show your face. You're hot on the case of London's latest

Jack the Ripper wannabe. Don't stay inside cooped up. Allow me to return the favor and disrupt your plans.

Eddie had seen the news reports calling him a copycat of the infamous Ripper. Of course, he disagreed with the association.

I'm nothing like him. He used a knife. What skill does that take? Breaking a person down by hand is entirely different. It's impossible to compare the two. But what can I expect from a news organization that cares more about views and likes as opposed to getting their facts straight? If they knew anything about MMA, they'd know I had to train hard and practice daily for me to do what I've done.

Eddie took a sip of his tea from the takeaway cup he was holding. He was thinking about breaking away from his surveillance to get something to eat when he spotted a familiar face across the street. It was Agent Gray. He'd just exited the building and was waiting near the road.

Where are you going? Do you have a lead? Is it pointing across the street from you? I don't think so because if it was, you would see me.

A vehicle came to a stop next to Gray, and he climbed inside.

It's your bobby partner, DI Gaston. Are you off to look for me? Good luck.

44

Alan Day was the investigator assigned to oversee the investigation at Eddie's home. He'd been working in forensics most of his law enforcement career and had partnered with Gaston on a few cases. Day was the only member of his team at the scene when Gaston called. He agreed to stick around until they arrived.

"Chi," Day called out from the doorway.

"Thanks, mate, for sticking around," Gaston said as he slapped Day on the arm. "This is Special Agent Gray. He's helping with the investigation."

"Are you enjoying your time here in London?" Day said as he shook Gray's hand.

"I was able to have a wonderful meal at the Black Forest. Amazing venison."

"Yes, that is a restaurant for meat lovers. The missus convinced me to give up meat three years ago. I'm one hundred percent plant-based."

"How's that working for you?"

"So far, it's great. I managed to drop five stones." Day patted his belly. "I believe that's about seventy pounds. I'm due to retire in six months, and the missus wants to make sure I have a long and healthy retirement."

"Congratulations. I wish you the best."

"Come inside," Day said as he glanced up. "The sky is getting dark. It might rain soon." Day closed the front door behind them. "I'm assuming you came back because of a thought."

Gaston quickly brought Day up to speed on Eddie being a twin.

"I thought I'd seen and heard it all, but twin serial killers? Who would have ever imagined?"

"We have the DNA match but nothing else to confirm," Gaston said. "But we have a few leads we're chasing down. We were hoping there might be something here that might suggest Eddie was in communication with Bowen."

"Well, officially, we're done here in the home. We collected a toothbrush from the bathroom in the master bedroom room and hair strands from a brush. We'll be able to cross-check the DNA profile from that with the blood sample pulled off the victim's shirt. We also lifted several prints from the bedroom. Sadly we didn't find any computers or tablets or a phone in the home. Either he took those items with him or didn't use them, which I highly doubt. There's a pile of mail on the kitchen counter if you want to sort through it."

"Anything interesting come up in the basement?" Gray asked.

"We were able to collect some DNA profiles, which I suspect will match the victims. There will be no room for doubt that Eddie is responsible for the murders. It's only a matter of apprehending him. Does Eddie share the same surname? Bowen?"

"We have yet to confirm that," Gaston said. "We believe Eddie is an alias. We haven't found anything yet that can confirm his name."

"I see. Do you mind if I take a look at that photo you have of Gary Bowen?"

Gray pulled up the picture on his phone.

Day removed a pair of reading glasses from the sport coat he wore and slipped them on. "So this is Eddie, or at least what he looks like." He peered at Gray and Gaston over the top of the glasses. "It'll be interesting to find out what really motivated them to do such gruesome things to innocent people."

"Clearly, the baggage they're carrying with them is damaged beyond repair," Gaston said.

Day chuckled. "I couldn't have said it better myself. Special Agent Gray, you're a profiler. I assume you've come across a lot of disturbed people. Have you seen anything like this before?"

"I haven't. I didn't get a chance to interview Gary Bowen. He was shot dead during apprehension. If it's possible, I hope we can bring Eddie in alive. We can learn a lot from interviewing him."

"Yes, I imagine you would." Day handed the phone back to Gray.

Just then, Day's phone rang. "Excuse me, it's the missus."

While Day was on his phone, Gray walked into the kitchen and sorted through the pile of mail. "I don't see anything other than utility bills and junk mail."

Gaston came up behind him. "I don't see a Wi-Fi unit in the house."

"I'm sure he's been on a burner phone."

"If he did have a desktop or laptop, he took it with him."

"I agree," Gray said. "You know what I find strange? The methods in which Eddie and Gary operated."

"What do you mean?"

"Eddie seemed more organized. He planned ahead and took steps to cover his tracks. Gary did nothing like that. To me, it looked like he was figuring it out as he went along."

"They both left bodies in a place where they could easily be discovered. I wonder if that was the point," Gaston said. "They wanted people to find them?"

"It's possible, but I think it's inexperience. But Eddie did seem to have it together a bit more, which supports my theory that he's a control freak. Gary had a goal he wanted to achieve. That gave him tunnel vision. Eddie wanted control, so he took steps to ensure he was in control of what he was doing and what the outcome would be."

"You'd think twin serial killers would kill in the same way, right?" Gaston said.

"That would be the conventional thinking, but I'm not an expert on twin behavior."

The two men headed downstairs for another look at the basement.

"They had to be talking," Gaston said. "The setup is nearly identical. They were just teaching different classes."

"I agree. The fact that they both opted to teach classes tells me they experienced the same childhood trauma, most likely some form of betrayal."

"Maybe they both had difficulty with school . . . bullies."

Gray nodded. "There's definitely a distrust of authority. I don't think we can discount physical or sexual abuse."

"I wonder why they taught different classes. You'd think twins would share the same interests."

"I'm not sure. I'm hoping the detectives back in Iowa can shed light on a lot of the questions you and I have."

"No response yet to your call?"

"Not yet."

"We still need to catch Eddie. How can we use this information?"

"With Eddie, I think the key is to make him think he's still in control and can carry on with his plan."

"You still want to bait him into the open."

"I do."

45

"Sterling. I'll admit I was surprised to hear your voice again," Detective Sparks said.

Gaston and Gray had wrapped up their tour of Eddie's home and were driving back to headquarters when Sparks called.

"Hi, Simon. I appreciate you getting back to me so quickly," Gray said as a crack of thunder erupted in the sky.

"No problem. Sounds like you're caught up in a nasty storm."

"It just started coming down hard a few seconds ago."

"What can I do for you?"

"You mind if we switch to video? I'm working an investigation in London, and it would be great if my colleague could be a part of the call."

"Sure. Not a problem."

Gray hung up and then started a video call. "Simon, this is DI Gaston with the Metropolitan Police. Detective Sparks is the detective I assisted in the Iowa investigation."

"Nice to make your acquaintance, DI Gaston. Special Agent Sterling was a great help to us. I hope he's equally helpful there."

"Yes, he is."

Gray quickly brought Sparks up to speed on the investigation he was working with the tie-in to Gary Bowen. Sparks took a moment to collect his thoughts before answering.

"Sterling, are you sure you got this right?"

"The DNA profile is a one hundred percent match. Only identical twins can pull that off. Plus, we have a victim that ID'd Bowen as her abductor. Not only that, you know those Jack the Ripper books we found in the home? Yeah, well, his brother here, we call him Eddie, also had the same reading material. Not only that: a bookmark being used by Eddie had the exact same handwritten wording on it as the framed quote in Bowen's home."

"You're saying she looked at Bowen's photo and was positive she was looking at your suspect there?"

"Yep. Another investigator showed the victim the photo without any explanation, and she identified Bowen as Eddie. Gary Bowen is Eddie's twin brother. We believe 'Eddie' is an alias. We also believe he might have used a disguise, and that's why security cam footage of him doesn't track. I definitely would have recognized a mirror image of Gary Bowen. This is why I'm calling. What do you know about Bowen's past?"

"If he has a twin brother, that's news to me. As far I knew, he was an only child. Both parents passed. I can double-check city records for death certificates and birth certificates."

"Is there anything you can think of that might explain this?" Gray asked.

"I can't claim to know everything about Bowen's past. Maybe he's got family that we don't know about. It's not unheard of for siblings to be separated at birth or one given up for adoption and it's kept secret. People do all sorts of strange things."

"You're right. Maybe having twins was too much for a young couple to care for. I'd also look for any evidence of him communicating with someone in London."

"Let me do some digging around and I'll get back to you."

"The sooner, the better. Eddie is on the run, and we don't think he's aware of what we know. If he does have extended family, there's a chance they could be here, or they might be able to help."

"I'll do what I can on my end to help you catch this guy. If he's anything like Gary Bowen, which he is from the sound of it, then he needs to be put down."

"I appreciate your help with this."

"No problem. Talk soon."

No sooner had Gray ended the call than the rain came down even harder, forcing Gaston to slow his vehicle.

"Welcome to London," Gaston said. "You enjoyed fairly nice weather the first couple of days. Now you'll get a taste of the dreariness. All we need is for the fog to roll in, and your London experience will be complete."

"Is London really that foggy?"

"Not so much now as it was when I was a little boy. But it does roll in from time to time. There's a chance it'll pay us a visit tonight."

The rain turned what should have been a forty-minute drive into an hour-and-fifteen-minute crawl across the city. Gray rubbed his hands together for warmth as the two walked across the underground parking lot toward the elevators. "It's a little colder today."

"The rain will do it," Gaston said as he pressed the call button. "Your comment about giving up a child for adoption might be what happened here," Gaston said. "Detective Sparks should be able to confirm that with birth records."

"That's what I'm hoping. We still have the problem of finding Eddie, though."

"Every bobby in the city has that photograph," Gaston said. "He can't stay hidden forever."

"Can't hurt to make the rounds at the MMA training gyms in the city and see if Eddie has shown his face around."

"I had the same thought." Gaston glanced at his watch. "I think we should interview Mia Thomas again. She's teaching a class tonight. Now that we have a positive ID on Eddie, she might have more useful information."

Gray walked over to the bulletin board and started looking at the screen grabs of men taking MMA classes at the gym. "We were wrong. The two individuals we liked weren't Eddie, not even the other one Lillie liked." He turned around, facing Gaston.

"I also already confirmed that there are no members with the first name Eddie or Edward on that list of registered members we received. He's got to be using an alias. Or there is the option that he never went to the gym. It is possible that his first three victims saw the cryptocurrency advertisement in another location."

"We might be placing too much importance on the gym."

Just as those words left Gray's mouth, a thought popped into his head, causing his gaze to drift off into the distance.

"Sterling. What is it?" Gaston asked.

"Remember that first day we visited the gym when we went back at night? I mentioned a member had bumped into me."

"Yeah, you said there was something about him that made you chase after him. You think that was Eddie?"

"It's got to be the only explanation. I couldn't pinpoint why at the time it gave me pause, but thinking back, that had to be it. I looked him straight in the eyes. That was Eddie."

Knowing he had bumped into Eddie his first day in London made the back of his neck tingle. Gray pulled up the photo of Gary Bowen on his phone and studied it.

"The eyes. That's what did it. Looking at it now, even the facial structure, chin, and cheeks—it's Bowen, except Eddie had muttonchops and a different eye color. But it's him. I'm positive."

Gaston came over and looked at the photo. "If that's true, then you're the only person to have seen both men."

"I can't freaking believe it. I bumped into the son of bitch my first day here."

Gaston's cell phone rang. "DI Gaston. Lillie, how's Evie? Good to hear. Sterling and I have everything under control. Take some time. Are you sure? It's not necessary. Okay. Cheers." Gaston pocketed his phone. "Lillie's on her way over here. She's angry."

"She okay?"

"She's fine, but her attention is back on Eddie. He pissed off the wrong woman."

46

Gray and Gaston decided to split up. Gaston would head back to the gym. Gray and Pratt would visit a few other MMA gyms. Gray definitely noticed a difference in Pratt's demeanor as they rode in a taxi to a nearby MMA training center.

"How's Evie doing?" he asked.

"She still has nightmares at night, but she seems to be calming down."

"What about her shifts at the hospital?"

"She's decided to take a week off. Her mind isn't where it needs to be to do her job."

"Makes sense. When she's ready, it'll be good for her to head back and keep herself occupied. Now for my second question: How are you doing? Where's your head at?"

Pratt looked directly into Gray's eyes. "The truth? I'm pissed. But I don't want you to worry about my decision-making skills. I'm completely focused. Do you want me to excuse myself from the investigation?"

"Not at all. I like the fire burning inside of you. Was that something you were thinking?"

"Not unless I'm ordered to."

"Good, because we need to catch the psycho. I realized earlier that I saw Eddie, actually bumped into him."

"When?"

"That night, Chi and I went back to speak to the instructor who taught the MMA classes at the gym. I bumped into a member who was in a hurry on the way out. Something about him stuck with me, enough that I decided to question him. I ran out after him, but he had already disappeared."

"You really think that was Eddie? Wouldn't it have been clear from the onset that he's an identical twin?"

"You'd think, but he was wearing a ball cap and had muttonchops. The shape of his eyes and cheekbones were the same. What I think threw me off was his eye color. Maybe the muttonchops as well. But studying Bowen's photo again, I'm sure that was Eddie. The eyes are what really did it for me."

"So, safe to say they don't dress and groom the same."

"They don't, and he also could be purposely disguising himself. It would make complete sense if they planned to do this together so that a connection wouldn't be made if either one was caught."

"You think Eddie knows his brother is dead?"

"I'm sure he does. I don't believe they independently came up with this scheme without talking. Before you arrived at headquarters, I spoke to one of the detectives back in Iowa. This is all new news to him as well. That's a whole lot of planning, for years, perhaps, to keep each other's existence a secret."

"Evie mentioned he didn't sound like a proper British person," Pratt said. "He might have moved here recently and picked up on our slang and intonations."

"I can see that being the case. I still find it hard to believe the detectives back in Iowa didn't know anything about Gary Bowen having a twin brother."

"It is, but if I'm to be blunt, I'm more concerned about apprehending this bloody bastard rather than figuring out his backstory. That's the training center over there." Pratt pointed.

Gray and Pratt hopped out of the taxi and ran the short distance to the building.

"Boy, the rain sure is holding steady," Gray said as he gave his forehead a wipe with the back of his hand. "At least it's been reduced to a drizzle."

"It'll probably last into the night," Pratt said.

The musty scent of a locker room hit them both as soon as they entered the gym. There must have been about twenty individuals training on the mats. In the center was an octagon ring with two fighters sparring while a coach called out instructions from the side. There were numerous heavy bags and speed bags along one side. The gym was also well equipped with free weights and exercise machines.

A man behind a counter near the entrance called out to them. "Welcome to Silva's MMA. Can I answer any questions for you? We're running a special right now. Ten percent off one month's membership."

Gray flashed the man his identification. "I'm Special Agent Gray. This is Ms. Pratt with Interpol. We'd like to speak to whoever is in charge here."

"That's Mr. Silva. I'll be right back."

A few moments later, a sweaty man wearing a traditional gi walked up to them. "I'm Jose Silva," he said with a Brazilian accent. "What's the problem?"

"No problem. Just a simple question: Has this man ever come here to train?"

Silva leaned in for a better look at the photo on Gray's phone. "No."

"You sure?"

"Yeah, I'm positive. I know everyone who trains here. This man was never here."

"Are most of your fighters here beginner or advanced?"

"Some beginner. Most of the men who train here have had a solid two years or more. We take on beginners, but only after we assess them. For most of them, we recommend another gym that's more suited for their level. A lot of them just want a good workout. If they're serious about MMA, they can always come back later."

"You mind giving us the name of that place?"

"It's called MMA Academy. It's in Soho, near the Oxford Circus Tube station."

Silva grabbed a pen and wrote the name and phone number down on the back of a flyer. "Is there anything else? I'm in the middle of a training session with my best fighter."

"That's all. We appreciate your time."

Gray and Pratt flagged another taxi and made their way over to the other training facility. When they arrived, they understood why Silva sent a lot of potential business here.

The large neon sign flashing the MMA Academy logo was more fitting for a nightclub. The clientele entering the place looked nothing like the blue-collar Rocky Balboa types at Silva's gym. These individuals were dressed in designer suits and fresh out of their upper management corporate jobs. They'd signed up for the latest workout trend, and in six months, they'd move on to the next trendy exercise.

Inside, club music blared from speakers, not what you would expect from an MMA gym. It smelled lemony fresh, and the reception area resembled more of a hotel than a gym. Gray quickly made the introductions, and he and Pratt waited for a manager. While they waited, they showed the photo of Bowen to the man and woman operating the reception counter. Both said they didn't recognize Bowen but also admitted they had just started two weeks prior.

"Hello, I'm the manager on duty today. How can I be of help?" the man said as he flashed his white veneers.

"Do you recall seeing this individual visit or train at your facility?" Gray asked.

"Do you mind if I have a closer look?" the manager asked. He zoomed in on Bowen's face. "I do recognize this man. He was here a while ago. At least six months ago. I haven't seen him since. I can check our files and see if he's still a member. What's his name?"

"We just know his first name," Gray said. "It's Eddie."

"No worries. I can do a search for Eddie. We take a photo of each client and attach it to their names."

The manager went behind the counter and tapped away on a computer. "Hmm, this is strange."

"Is there a problem?" Gray asked.

"I have an Eddie in the system, but the photo doesn't match the one you have. Come take a look."

Gray and Pratt went over to the other side of the counter and looked at the screen.

"Yeah, that's not our Eddie. Is there any chance you missed him during the search?"

The manager shook his head. "Anyone with that name would have appeared."

"He probably gave a different name when registering," Pratt said.

"Seems like it," Gray turned to the manager. "But you're sure this man was a client here?"

"I'm positive. If he did give another name, he's in the database, but we have thousands of clients. It'll take a long time to search manually through the photos. But I'm pretty sure it's been more than six months since I've seen him in here. And I know he trained with Alexei. Those are fairly advanced courses."

"Is Alexei here? I'd like to speak with him, if it's possible."

"Sure. Let me track him down."

"I hope Alexei can shed some light on Eddie," Pratt said.

A few minutes later, a tall white man approached them. "I'm Alexei," he said with a noticeable Russian accent. "You have some questions for me?"

"We understand you trained this individual. His name was Eddie."

Alexei looked at the photo. "Yes, I train him. But his name is not Eddie. His name is Gary."

Gray gave Pratt a quick look. "Gary? We thought it was Eddie. Are you positive it was Gary?"

"That's what he told me. I call people whatever name they give me."

"Did you learn his surname?"

Alexei shook his head.

"What kind of student was he? Nice? Quiet? Aggressive? What can you tell us about him?"

"He was quiet but always look angry. His skills were okay. He had training before he came here, but the problem I have with him is he doesn't listen. I try to correct some bad habits with his technique, but he don't believe me. He like to argue. Not just with me, but with other fighters. I tell him he need to calm down."

"What happened then?"

Alexei shrugged. "After a while, he never come back."

"I see. Did you learn anything about his social life, like whether he had a girlfriend, or places he likes to hang out, or interests?"

"He not mention a girlfriend to me, but when I assess his skill level, I ask him where he train before. He tell me in America."

"Where in America?"

"He only tell me he train in American dojos."

"Did he mention why he came to London?"

"No."

"From his skill level, do you think he's capable of seriously hurting people?"

"If his opponent is trained at some level, no. But if a person has no training, yes."

"He sounds like a bully," Pratt said. "I get the impression you didn't care much for him."

"He is a client. Does not matter if I like him. My job is to train him."

"Did he come and leave alone? Did he mention friends?"

"I not pay attention to him outside of our class, but he talk about the East End of London a couple of times."

"What about it?" Gray asked.

Alexi shrugged. "He tell me he like that area and asked if I go there. I said no."

"What part of the East End?" Pratt asked.

"Whitechapel."

47

Alexei had nothing more to offer about Eddie. Still, outside of Evie, he knew more about Eddie than anybody else that had been questioned.

"He used the name Gary at the gym. That's his brother's name," Gray said as he and Pratt exited the building. "It's one more thing that connects the two."

"It is, but that's not the most interesting thing to come out of Alexei's mouth. Whitechapel was."

"What's with Whitechapel?"

"Aside from being an area in the East End, it's where the Jack the Ripper murders took place."

Gray stopped in his tracks. "You're kidding, right?"

"No. Why? Does that change the profile?"

"No, but both men had a collection of Jack the Ripper books. How far away are we from there?"

"About a twenty-minute ride in a cab. Do you want to go there?"

"We don't have any leads on where Eddie might be. Maybe he's got a place there, or there's a gym or coffee shop that he hangs out at. I mean, Jack the Ripper. That alone is enough to merit a visit."

"There's a Jack the Ripper museum near Whitechapel. Obviously, there are the murder sites, though many have been developed over. If I recall correctly, there might even be a self-guided walking tour." Pratt took out her phone and did a search. "Here we go. It's an audio tour that you download to your phone. It's about five kilometers long and takes about two and a half hours with fourteen stops."

"We should check in with Chi and see if he's discovered anything worthy," Gray said before making a call. "Chi, it's Sterling. Anything fruitful on your end?"

"I just got done talking to Mia. She said she doesn't recognize Gary Bowen. That means she never saw Eddie."

"We found a gym that Eddie trained at."

Gray told Gaston everything they'd learned from Alexei.

"Excellent," Gaston said. "Alexei and the manager on duty had no problem identifying Gary Bowen as Eddie?"

"Not one bit. I still think Eddie used a disguise at Fitness World. It had been eight months since he last trained at MMA Academy. During that time, he could have been planning, which included disguising for himself. Outside of Jack the Ripper, does Whitechapel spark a thought in your head?" Gray asked.

"It doesn't," Gaston answered. "Are you guys heading there?"

"We were thinking of doing the walking tour, it starts at the Whitechapel Tube station. Alexei said Eddie mentioned the East End of London multiple times. Lillie made the connection to Whitechapel. I don't know if anything will come out of it. But it's a lead. Eddie might have romanticized what Jack the Ripper did or represented. It could be what put him on the path that he and his brother were on."

"I'll meet up with you two over there," Gaston said.

Gray ended the call. "Chi is meeting us. It might be faster if we each took a section of the tour."

After spotting Gray exit the Metropolitan Police, Eddie had followed him and the DI back to his home in Maida Vale. He was a little let down that they'd returned to the house. *They must not have had any strong leads if they're coming back to pick over the crumbs. You'll find nothing of substance in there. I never treated that place like a home, only a place to rest my head. Maybe Agent Gray isn't all that great.*

Eddie had felt confident the agent and the DI were no closer to catching him when they'd left his home. He'd even thought of taking the night off but decided it was much more fun following the dynamic duo. He was happy he did because Agent Gray had taken on a new partner: the woman who had rushed to Evie's rescue. Eddie had no idea who she was and simply figured she was another DI working the investigation. But it was a no-brainer to follow them and not DI Gaston. When they led Eddie to Silva's MMA, Eddie had to reconsider his previous thoughts on Gray. Even more so when their next stop was the MMA Academy.

Gray and Pratt arrived at the Whitechapel Tube station first. It was still drizzling, and as Gaston had foretold, a light fog drifted across the city.

"What a night to be out," Pratt said.

"It's a bit eerie, isn't it?"

"To say the least."

While they waited for Gaston, they downloaded the self-guided walking tour and studied the route. There were fourteen stops; eleven were marked by the alphabet. The other three stops were the Whitechapel Gallery, the East London Mosque, and the Royal London Hospital.

"Stops marked by the alphabet form a loop," Gray said as he stared at his phone. "Maybe you and I work backward from K to F, and Gaston can take A to E."

"We'll end up meeting in the middle," Pratt said. "Since we have six stops, maybe we can get started and just tell Gaston to take the other route."

Before setting off, Gray sent Gaston a text message letting him know what he and Pratt were doing. They both had their phones out with the audio turned up. Stop K was the last stop on the walking tour, and it was a pub.

"Nice way to end the tour," Gray said.

They peeked inside and looked over the crowd. Eddie wasn't there. Gray showed the two bartenders a photo of Bowen, and neither of them recognized him. After a few more minutes of looking the place over, they left and moved to the next stop: J.

The audio navigated to a modern building on the corner of Bell Lane and White's Row. The site of Jack the Ripper's fifth victim: Mary Jane Kelly.

The audio went on to tell them that Dorset Street, where Mary's body was found, used to be where the building now sits.

"Did you know that?" Gray asked.

"I did. Dorset Street was arguably the most dangerous street in all of London when Mary was living. I believe the street was built over about ten years ago."

Just then, Gray received a text message from Gaston stating that he had started the walking tour in the opposite direction.

"Gaston's on the move," Gray said. "We should get going."

The next stop was literally a building across the street. According to the audio, it was an old workhouse, which was a place where the poor were offered room and board in exchange for performing manual labor.

"The disabled, the orphaned, or the elderly with no family often ended up in these places," Pratt said. "This entire area was like a lawless slum. It's probably what made it so easy for Jack the Ripper to prey on the prostitutes in the area. You think that means anything for Eddie?"

"It might just be as simple as a control issue. One of the theories for the Ripper was that he believed his son died from contracting an STD from a prostitute. If that's true, killing prostitutes was a way of cleansing the area of the infection. You know the Ripper's victims were cut open. So were Bowen's. Eddie didn't cut his victims open, but he did break them apart. All three carried out body mutilation."

"I don't think I want to dive any deeper into Eddie's frame of mind," Pratt said. "I know enough to conclude that he's a lunatic that needs to be behind bars for the rest of his life."

Gray and Pratt walked down Bell Lane. It was quiet and devoid of foot traffic other than them. The drizzle was still falling, annoying Gray and dampening his jeans. To make matters worse, the fog had thickened. He zipped up his windbreaker and shoved one hand into his pocket while the other held his phone. Pratt had a hood attached to her windbreaker and had already pulled it tight over her head.

"I should have known better," she said, "and brought an umbrella."

"It's just a little water. It won't kill us."

"I'm surprised by the fog. It normally doesn't get like this."

Gray drew in a deep breath. "London fog. One more thing I've gotten a chance to experience."

48

Eddie stood in the shadows at the corner of Bell Lane and White's Row as he watched Gray and the woman. *How romantic. A walking tour of Jack the Ripper's past, though I hope you know you're doing it backward. I've done it many times. If you follow the audio guide, it's obvious. But I guess you two are like my brother: stubborn. You have to do things your way, even if it's the wrong way. As much as I think you two make a lovely couple, I'm sorry, darling; I'm not interested in a threesome. Only Agent Gray's invited to my class.*

Eddie stuck close to the building, careful not to get too close. Bell Lane was quiet and dark. Given the fog that night, it would have been a perfect opportunity for Eddie to teach Gray a lesson, especially after Bell Lane turned into Goulston Street. Eddie was familiar with that area. The shops there would be closed at that hour, and there were no eateries, pubs, or cafés along that stretch. It would have been perfect for an ambush.

I'm sure if Jack were here today, he would have thought the exact same thing. Great minds think alike.

Right before the street narrowed and changed over to Goulston, there was a tiny pub. Everything past that was a ghost town. Gray and the woman had stopped, and she headed in while he waited outside.

Can this be my lucky day? Can it really? She's gone inside to use the toilet. I have a couple of minutes before she returns. The agent was occupied with his phone and had his back facing Eddie. The excitement made Eddie's heart beat a little faster.

He won't see me coming. Don't blow it. You have the advantage. Bring the big bad agent down. Eddie pulled his ball cap lower.

Gray's phone rang. It was Gaston calling.

"Chi, how are things on your end?"

"I've made it past two locations on this walking tour, but to be honest, I'm not sure what I'm looking for."

"We just know that Eddie talked a lot about this area. Maybe he has another place here, or he frequents a pub in the area. It's possible there's a fascination with Jack the Ripper."

"London is a big city. Eddie could be anywhere. Where are you two now?"

"We're on Bell Lane. Lillie stepped into a pub to use the restroom."

Just then a man in a ball cap walked past Gray, brushing against his arm.

"Excuse me," Gray said.

"What's happening?" Gaston asked.

"Nothing, just accidentally bumped into someone."

The passing man glanced back over his shoulder and mumbled something to Gray.

"What's that?" Gray called out.

"Is he taking the piss out of you?" Gaston asked.

"Not sure. Don't worry about it. We'll see you in a bit."

Gray disconnected the call as he watched the man continue down the dark lane until he disappeared in the fog. A beat later, he heard a voice yell out.

"You can't stop me, Agent Gray!"

Pratt exited the pub while on the phone with Evie. "I think we'll be here another hour. Yes, I promise I'll come as soon as we finish up here."

She looked around, wondering where Gray had gone, and assumed he must have ducked inside to use the loo. She read and answered emails on her phone while she waited. But after a while, it dawned on her that Gray had been gone longer than expected. She headed back inside to look around the pub, thinking he might have had a seat while waiting for her, but he was nowhere to be seen. Pratt rang Gray's phone, but he didn't answer.

She knocked on the men's bathroom door, but there was no answer. Shortly after, a man exited, and she asked him if there was anyone else inside. To which he replied no.

Hmmm, where is he?

Pratt headed back outside. It was still drizzling, and the fog seemed thicker than she remembered.

Did you go for a walk?

"Sterling!" She waited a moment before calling his name once more. But there was no response.

It's a bit peculiar for him to simply wander off.

She tried ringing Gray's phone again, but there was still no answer. She then rang Gaston, thinking maybe they somehow met up.

"Chi, it's Lillie. Is Sterling with you? He's not here. I had stepped into a pub to use the loo, but when I came back out, he was gone. I already checked. He's not in there. You did? What did you talk about? I see. There was. Who was he? Maybe he did. I'm heading south on Bell Lane, right where it turns into Goulston. Right. See you."

Gaston had mentioned that a man had bumped into Gray, and maybe he went after him. Pratt continued down Goulston. All of the shops were closed, and only the clickity-clack of her shoes could be heard.

Pratt called out for Sterling before trying him on his phone again. In both instances, she was met with silence. And to be honest, the silence worried her.

49

Son of a bitch! Gray wasted no time running down Goulston after the man who had brushed up against him. Only one person in London would ever utter those five words: *You can't stop me, Gray.*

It's Eddie. He's been following me. Maybe Eddie and his brother had been talking regularly. But how did Gary Bowen know who I was?

It didn't really matter how Eddie had discovered Gray's identity. The important thing was that Gray knew what would bait Eddie out into the open: himself.

Not sure if Eddie was lurking in the shadows or if he was even armed. Gray slowed his pace. He should have waited for Pratt, but he knew that's not what Eddie was after. He would simply disappear if Gray and Pratt chased after him. For some reason, the serial killer wanted him. And only him.

Maybe he thinks I killed his brother.

With his ears peeled for the slightest movement, Gray walked down the center of the road, every so often blinking the drizzling rain from his eyes. A combination of the fog and a lack of streetlamps didn't help matters. But Gray figured if he couldn't see Eddie, the same went for him.

"Big bad Agent Gray," a voice called out.

Gray froze.

He's near, maybe twenty to thirty feet away. He's definitely ahead of me. Can he see me?

"Come out, Eddie," Gray called out as he took a step forward. "It's just the two of us. Isn't that what you wanted?"

"I'm not like my brother," Eddie called out again. "He was always the weaker one."

"That's already been made clear to me. You've thought things through. Gary wasn't as organized. That was his downfall."

"He liked to blame others for his inefficiencies."

"And you don't?"

Eddie laughed. "I don't crave anyone's approval. My brother did. That's the difference between us."

"I get it. You're your own man. But let me ask you one thing. What kind of man picks on women who can't defend themselves against a trained fighter?"

"You don't get it, do you? I wasn't picking on them. I was punishing them for their insubordination. Their inability to follow commands."

"You stated you don't seek validation from others, but it seems to me you demand others seek it from you. That's the funny thing about this. You get angry when they don't listen to you. Do you know what that tells me? You do want their validation. You want them to acknowledge you. I'm sorry to say, Eddie, you and your brother are no different. You're both angry at the way others have viewed you two."

No sooner had those words left Gray's mouth than a blur of movement appeared at the edge of his peripheral vision—not enough time to deflect the blow from Eddie's fist.

Gray was struck hard in the side of the head, sending him walking sideways in a slight daze. He quickly collected himself, fists up, ready for another attack, but Eddie had disappeared.

"You keep proving my point, Eddie. You can only win in life if you give yourself an advantage. You're not as good as you think. Maybe that's why others have judged you. You're arrogant."

This time Eddie moved in from behind Gray, but he'd heard the footsteps and spun quickly enough to deflect Eddie's rapid strikes. With his forearms up, Gray backed away while moving his head side to side. He connected with a snapping punch to Eddie's chin.

Gray moved in with a tight right hook, but Eddie read his move and backed away in time, disappearing into the fog once more. All of Gray's senses were on high alert as he spun around, searching for Eddie. He assumed the pop shots Eddie was taking were to simply assess Gray's abilities. Also, Gray still wasn't sure if Eddie had a weapon on him.

"What do you say, Eddie? Do you want to settle this mano a mano? A good old-fashioned bare-knuckle brawl in the streets of London. I'm curious to see how skilled of a fighter you are."

"You think you can out-fight me?" Eddie called. "Pathetic."

Eddie had moved farther down the Goulston.

"A little premature to go around claiming to be a fighter. I think your skills have yet to be seriously tested," Gray said as he moved toward Eddie's voice.

"Wouldn't you like to know?"

Eddie's voice came from the left. It sounded like he had moved from Goulston to a small alleyway, perhaps. Gray proceeded cautiously with fists up in front. He moved over to the building on his left and followed alongside until he reached the corner. Still, when he tried to turn, he bumped into a metal barrier, a security arm gate. But that was definitely where he thought he had heard Eddie's voice.

The single security arm was only three feet above the pavement, and Gray stepped over it one leg at a time. He moved forward slowly until he reached an iron gate. The spacing between the pickets was too narrow for anybody to slip between, even a child. Gray turned back around and found himself face-to-face with Eddie.

50

———

Before Gray could react, Eddie had shot forward for a takedown. Both of his arms wrapped around Gray's legs as his shoulder slammed into Gray, forcing him back and off his feet. Gray landed on the pavement hard, sending a flash of pain rocketing up his back.

As Eddie moved forward to mount Gray, he clamped his arms around Eddie and pulled him down against his chest to stop him. He wrapped his legs around Eddie's back and held on, immobilizing him. But it left his head and face vulnerable to fist strikes.

Eddie took advantage of the hole in Gray's defense and struck the left side of Gray's face. Gray raised a forearm to protect himself, but Eddie's strikes were still getting through. Gray gripped harder with his legs and retaliated with blows from his free hand, slamming his fist into Eddie's face.

Eddie hooked his arm around Gray's free arm and rolled off him while slipping a leg under Gray's head and clamping his other over his chest. Gray knew precisely what move Eddie was attempting: an armbar. If that happened, Gray could say goodbye to his arm.

Gray yanked and twisted his arm as he squirmed, forcing Eddie to lose his grip on Gray's wrist.

"You can't win, Gray," Eddie said. "I have better training than you."

Eddie clamped down on Gray's wrist and started to extend Gray's arm.

He had to stop him. Gray turned his head and bit down on the soft flesh of Eddie's inner thigh right through his pants.

Eddie let out a yell and relaxed his grip. Gray yanked his arm free and swung his leg up, kicking Eddie's head. It was a glancing blow, but Eddie felt it as he yelled out once again, and Gray could move away from Eddie.

Gray got to his knees, but Eddie quickly wrapped his legs around Gray's waist, stopping him from standing. He pulled down and reached an arm around the back of Gray's neck to close the distance between them.

Eddie's ball cap had slipped off his head. Their faces were only inches apart. The resemblance between Eddie and his brother was apparent, except for one thing. Gray bit down on Eddie's nose and pulled back, tearing off the prosthetic. He spit it out.

"Surprise!" Eddie shouted.

Gray laid into Eddie with multiple fist strikes, but Eddie had by then gained control of Gray's head and held it to his chest. Eddie was much more effective guarding himself than Gray had anticipated and was deflecting most of Gray's blows. Gray moved to body strikes, but Eddie clamped his legs higher on Gray's back, limiting his range. Rabbit punches, at best, were all Gray could deliver.

Gray had underestimated Eddie's skill level. He was more than capable of causing severe damage, maybe even killing him. But Gray had one advantage: his strength. Eddie might be a more skilled grappler than he was, but Gray was also no slouch when it came to hand-to-hand combat. Gray lifted Eddie off the ground and slammed him back down.

Again.

And again.

Eddie's legs lost their grip around Gray's body, giving Gray more movement. He struck Eddie with two horizontal elbow strikes. Eddie countered with elbow strikes of his own, but Gray had already freed himself from Eddie's grips and gotten to his feet by then. Eddie rolled away and quickly stood up in time to fend off Gray's punches. Gray continued his assault, backing Eddie toward the building behind him.

Eddie countered with stinging low kicks to Gray's outer thigh, but Gray sucked it up and continued to strike, catching Eddie with a solid punch to his face. Eddie stumbled but soon recovered with another low kick to the same spot on Gray's thigh. That one was too much for Gray, and his left leg buckled, causing him to drop to a knee.

Eddie hopped over the security arm. Gray took a moment to get to his feet and climbed over the security arm, but by then, Eddie had disappeared.

Dammit!

Gray started down Goulston when he heard a voice call his name. It was Pratt.

"Sterling," Pratt called out again.

"I'm over here. Follow the sound of my voice."

A few moments later, Pratt appeared, and Gray walked toward her, favoring his left leg.

"Are you okay?" she asked, looking him up and down.

"I'm fine, I'm fine. Eddie's here. He ran off right before you called out."

"Are you sure you're okay?"

"No, really, I'm fine. If anything, my ego is bruised. Eddie is well trained in MMA. We need to be careful."

"Maybe I should call a medic."

"Seriously, I'm fine. We need to go after him." Gray shook his leg. "See? Good as new. Come on."

Gray started off, but after a few steps, he stopped and groaned. "Damn. Those leg kicks killed."

"You need to give it a rest," Pratt said. "It's probably bruised. Look, I spoke with Chi not long ago. He's heading straight here. He should be arriving soon. I want to see if I can find Eddie."

"No, it's not safe. If he gets the jump on you . . . He's well trained is what I mean. Trust me."

"Agent Gray, is your girlfriend here to fight your battle for you?" Eddie called out from the fog.

"That bloody bastard." Pratt spun around. A beat later, she ran off.

"No, Lillie! Wait!"

Gray gritted his teeth and ran after Pratt. He couldn't see her, but he could hear her footsteps ahead of him.

"Lillie, where are you?"

But Pratt didn't answer the question. Instead, she screamed.

51

Gray heard signs of a struggle. He picked up the pace, doing his best to ignore the pain that shot through his leg with every step.

"Eddie. It's me you want. Leave her alone."

Whatever movement he had heard had suddenly ceased. Then, the outline of a man appeared. A few more steps, and Gray recognized Eddie standing over a body. It was Pratt.

"Do you still doubt my skills, Agent Gray?" Eddie said with a low growl.

Gray couldn't tell whether Pratt was dead or unconscious. She was lying on her side, motionless, with her back to Gray.

"You've just made your situation worse," Gray said.

"The cat is already out of the bag. How much worse can it be? We both know why we're standing here. The question we should be asking each other is, who will walk away?"

"I'll tell you right now. It's not going to be you."

"Opinions are like assholes. Everybody has one."

At that moment, Gray saw a striking difference between Eddie's and Gary's personalities. Even though he had only had a small opportunity to speak with Gary, he didn't sense entitlement or arrogance. Nor did the people he had interviewed who knew Gary mentioned that about him.

They'd always positioned him as quiet, a bit strange, and someone who kept to himself.

"Aside from your looks, you sound nothing like your brother."

"Are you analyzing me? I'll save you the trouble. My brother and I are different in every way. He's like a shadow, in that he's a replica of me, but that's about it."

"You're both killers."

"Like I said, a replica. He's a copycat who is always trying to be like his big brother."

"So this was all your idea? And your brother wanted to be like you, so he copied what you were doing?"

"As much as I would like to take credit for that, it wasn't my idea. There was a time when we were young, my brother and I lived under the same roof. Our foster father, caretaker, mentor, teacher, sick bastard, whatever, taught us everything we know."

"What are you talking about?"

"Do you need everything spelled out to you? However did you get your job? We were raised in the foster care system. We shared the same roof for a year. That's it."

"It explains why you two are so different in many ways, but the same. But that's not the clarification I was seeking. What did you mean by 'taught'?"

"Of course, yes. You're a profiler. You would be interested in that detail. We learned from him. Maybe he saw the same tendencies in us, but one day he brought us in on his secret, his desire to dissect women. He was a perfectionist. He was never caught, and don't bother searching for him. He's dead. But you're right in that my brother and I are different, which is strange for twins, but we're the same in every way when it comes to the hunger we share."

"This wasn't your first time killing, was it?"

"No, it wasn't, but it was mostly animals at first. But you know that, Agent Gray. Isn't that how individuals like me progress?"

"If you had not done this, Gary wouldn't have either? You said he's a copycat."

"As much as I want credit for that, it wasn't all my doing. For all I know, maybe he already had a few kills under his belt. I never asked. I never cared. We found out a few years ago that our Ripper father had left a bounty to us, but we had to compete for it. First one to kill five women wins the money."

"The quote. Gary had it framed. You used it as a bookmark."

"He had it framed? He was always the more idealistic one. But he was always the jealous one as well. It's why he snitched on me."

"You think I interviewed him, and he snitched, and that's how I found you?"

Eddie bounced his head from side to side. "What else could it be? I tried my best to teach him how to be more organized and not sloppy. I knew he would get caught and I would win."

This time it was Gray's turn to laugh. "Gary wasn't the sloppy one. You were. We got your DNA from blood splatter on Evie's shirt. That's how we connected you to your brother, Gary. If it weren't for that, we wouldn't be standing right here right now. All those precautions you took to conceal your identity at the gym and the coffee shops, the fake names you used, and the living arrangement you made with the owner of the house, all of it for naught because you let your guard down, and Evie got the jump on you. You blew it. I hate to rain on your parade, but you also got caught. You and your brother are exactly alike. Both of you are losers, but he was better."

"You're lying! He led you to me. There had to be something."

"Nope. Your brother was fairly buttoned up. It's the reason why local law enforcement requested the assistance of the FBI. That's how good you brother was."

"I don't believe you. I know Gary."

"No, you don't. You know nothing of him. You're just an arrogant, inse-cure bully. You like to think you're better than your brother, but you're not. You're the one who screwed up. You're responsible for getting caught. Not Gary. Get off your soapbox and face the consequences."

Gray balled his fists and quickly closed the distance. Eddie backed away but not quickly enough to avoid a strike to his face. Gray continued his assault, but Eddie countered with a leg kick to Gray's torso, backing him off.

Eddie went on the offensive, shooting for a takedown, but Gray quickly scooted back, avoiding Eddie's grasp. Gray sprawled his legs and fell forward on top of Eddie. He hooked both of his arms around Eddie's neck and fell backward to the ground, pulling Eddie down with him.

With his arms snug around Eddie's neck and his head tucked securely under the armpit, Gray moved Eddie into his guard by wrapping his legs around Eddie's torso. Gray then pushed down with his legs while pulling up with his arms.

The guillotine choke will render its victim unconscious in an average of nine seconds by cutting off blood circulation to the brain. But Gray was well aware that most of the pressure he was applying was on Eddie's trachea, cutting off his air, not his blood flow.

Eddie kicked his legs while blasting his fist into the side of Gray's head to break free. But Gray had a solid lock on Eddie's neck. Eddie's strikes slowed, and the force behind each punch lessened. His legs jerked once before falling limp.

Gray continued to squeeze, long past twenty seconds. "Not this time, pal. You're done."

52

"Sterling!"

Gray had just released Eddie from his grasp when Gaston showed up.

"Check on Lillie," Gray said. "I don't know her condition."

Gaston dropped down next to Pratt and checked her vitals. "Still breathing. She has a pulse." He shook her gently. "Lillie. Come on, dear. Wake up."

After a moment or two, Lillie's eyelids fluttered, and she regained consciousness.

"What happened?" she mumbled.

"Everything's fine. You're okay," Gaston said as he removed a handkerchief from his pocket and wiped her face dry.

"Eddie's here," Pratt said as he tried to sit up. "We need to stop him."

Gaston glanced at Eddie's motionless body. "Don't worry about him. He's been taken care of."

"Where's Sterling?" she asked.

"Lillie, I'm okay," Gray said as he came over to her. "How do you feel?"

"A little light-headed, but other than that, I'm okay. What happened?"

"I think Eddie put you in a chokehold, causing you to lose consciousness."

Gaston stood up, walked over to Eddie, and checked his vitals before making a call.

"Is he dead?" Pratt asked as she looked at Eddie.

"Yes," Gray said. "Come on, let's get you to your feet." Gray helped Pratt stand and steadied her. "Are you okay?"

"Really, I'm fine." She looked over at Eddie once more. "I don't remember him choking me. I only remember bumping into someone." Pratt looked back at Gray. "Are you sure it's him?"

"Positive."

"I want a closer look."

Pratt walked over to Eddie and knelt down beside him. He was lying on his back with his eyes closed and his mouth slightly agape.

"What happened to his nose?" Pratt asked as she looked up at Gray.

"That's a piece of the prosthetic he was wearing. I bit it off."

"You bit his nose?" A smile formed on Pratt's face as she stood up.

"Hey, this guy was a skilled grappler. Better than I'd anticipated. I did what I needed to do."

Gaston got off his phone. "I called it in. The cavalry is on its way." Gaston smiled as he gave Gray and Pratt each a pat on the shoulder. "We did it, mates. It's done."

"It is," Gray said.

The three of them stared at Eddie lying on the pavement. Gray couldn't help but wonder if it would have been better if Eddie were alive. The obvious reason: To study his mind. And then take that learning and apply it to future investigations. Of course, there was no guarantee that Eddie would have cooperated unless there was something in it for him. Attention from the media wouldn't do it. Eddie wasn't driven by fame.

"You okay, Sterling?" Gaston asked as he lowered his head to catch Gray's gaze.

"Yeah, I'm fine."

"Hey, you did what you needed to do, right? If you didn't take him out, he would have ended you. And at the time, you weren't sure of Lillie's condition. I would have done the same thing."

Gray nodded.

"Don't worry about anything. Lillie and I both have your back on this one. Eddie was a maniac."

A couple of nearby bobbies arrived and helped preserve the crime scene until CSI could take over. Gaston wanted everything done correctly. No mistakes. This was a big catch. He knew it would make the news, and his supervisors would scrutinize everything to be sure it was done by the books and nothing could come back to burn them. The politics in London were the same as anywhere. It didn't really matter that the killer was caught. What mattered more was how things were perceived after the fact. Gray completely understood where Gaston was coming from and supported him wholeheartedly.

Pratt left shortly after, wanting to get back to Evie. Plus, there was really no reason for her to stick around for that part of the investigation. The same went for Gray, but he didn't feel like leaving Gaston alone. It was a little after eleven that night when Gaston called it a wrap.

"I appreciate you being here," he said.

"I wanted to see it through, just like you did."

"The night's still young. You fancy a pint?"

"You read my mind."

"Brilliant. I know a pub in the neighborhood."

"I don't doubt that."

Gray and Gaston were sitting in a pub, downing cask ale, then munching on chips a little later.

"You still haven't told me how it all went down. Probably a good thing for us to be on the same page," Gaston said.

Gray walked Gaston through the series of events, starting with their conversation while Gray was waiting for Pratt outside the pub.

"You're kidding me?" A surprised look appeared on Gaston's face. "He actually shouted that out?"

"Yep. Clear as day. He said, 'You can't stop me, Agent Gray.'"

"Cheeky bastard, isn't he, to say that?"

"Remember that bookmark with the writing on it?"

"Yeah."

"It was from a letter from his foster father." Gray went on to fill Gaston in on Eddie and Gary's upbringing.

"The foster parent was a serial killer? You're kidding, right?"

"I wish I were. They were both groomed, and apparently even after leaving, there had to be contact. The letter is proof of that. According to Eddie, he was never caught. He's dead now, but I am curious to know who he was."

Gaston ran a hand through his hair. "Crazy world we live in. I'll tell you the truth; I would have loved to be involved in that punch-up after hearing this. Bloody bastard deserved everything he got."

"He was a skilled fighter. Those women had no chance against him. Even Evie was lucky. Getting the jump on Eddie saved her life."

"Lillie teaching her those moves saved her life."

"No doubt." Gray raised his pint and then continued with his account of what happened.

"At one point, he had me in an armbar. He was close to snapping my arm, but I was stronger than him and able to twist my arm free from his grip. That's when I knew things were serious. I have extensive training in hand-to-hand combat, and I always thought my grappling skills were sufficient—"

"They are sufficient. Saved your life back there," Gaston said. "I bet Eddie was just as surprised by your abilities as you were with his. I don't think he ever took on an opponent that was on par with him. Guys like Eddie build themselves up by picking on the weak."

"You're right about that."

"So how about telling me how it ended?" Gaston said.

"Guillotine choke."

"The best way to render someone unconscious." Gaston smiled. "But sometimes things don't always work out that way, do they?"

53

The following day, Gray felt refreshed and well rested. That had been his first decent sleep since arriving in London. He had texted his supervisor, Cooper, the night before to give him a heads-up that they'd caught the killer. He also added that a full report would be emailed to him the following morning. Cooper responded with a thumbs-up and his standard reply, *I knew I could count on you.*

Room service had just delivered a pot of black coffee along with cut fruit and plain yogurt. Already showered and ready for the day, Gray's plan was to type up the report and email it to Cooper before meeting with Gaston at headquarters. Gray had woken up that morning to a message from Gaston informing him that his supervisor wanted to meet. He had questions, but Gaston assured Gray that it was all a formality. Gray had already planned on heading into the station anyway.

After an hour of banging away on his laptop, Gray sent off the report, feeling proud of his contribution. He was getting ready to walk out the door when he received a message from Green. He hadn't heard a peep from her since her last message. Gray was caught a bit off guard. He had accepted the fact that Green would be moving on. But her message suggested otherwise. She stated she was looking forward to seeing him.

That's an interesting turn of events. Maybe there is hope for our relationship.

Gray responded, letting her know that he was wrapping up the investigation and returning stateside soon. He anticipated another day or two in London, but kept that assumption to himself. He couldn't foresee any work-related reason for him to remain any longer. And anyway, he was sure Cooper already had something else lined up for him.

When Gray arrived at the station, he found Gaston standing at his bulletin board, taking down the information.

"Good morning, Chi," Gray said.

"Good morning to you too. It's a beautiful day, isn't it?"

"It sure is. There's no better feeling than post-investigation wrap-up. Is Lillie coming in today?"

"She'll also be in the same meeting." Gaston glanced at his watch. "She should be in soon."

"Good morning," Pratt sang out as she appeared.

"Well, that makes three of us in a wonderful mood this morning," Gray said.

"I can't think of a better way to start the day than by successfully closing an investigation. Sterling, Chi, I wanted to let you both know that I gave each of you glowing reviews in my report to my superiors as well as yours. Sterling, I know this is our first time working together, but I'd like to go on record and say I hope it's not the last."

"Thank you, Lillie. You didn't need to do that," Gray said.

"Oh yes, I did. I know all too well that the actual people working an investigation don't get nearly enough credit."

"Well, since we're getting all mush and gushy . . ." Gray pretended to wipe away tears from his eyes. "I couldn't have asked for better partners. Here's to the three musketeers."

Pratt snapped a finger. "Oh! That reminds me. Evie and I would love it if you two came over to dinner tonight—if you don't have other plans. We need to celebrate."

"Count me in," Gray said.

"Same here," Gaston said.

Just then, Gaston's direct supervisor, DCI John Holt, entered the room. "Good morning, everyone. We're ready for you."

"Who's 'we?'" Gray whispered to Gaston. "I thought we were just meeting with Holt."

"Change of plans, I guess."

All three of them followed Holt to a conference room. Gathered around a long rectangular table were a lot of uniformed men that Gray had never seen before—except one, Boyd Hall, the DSU.

"DI Gaston, Special Agent Gray, Ms. Pratt," Hall said. "Thank you for being here today. Please take a seat."

There were no introductions of the others who had gathered. In Gray's experience, that usually meant it was all business, and it might not be fun.

"This is just an informal inquiry regarding the investigation. Nothing serious," Holt said. "We are here to clarify the details of the physical force used in apprehending the suspect, which resulted in this individual's death. We have read the reports of the three of you. Special Agent Gray, your supervisor was kind enough to forward your report directly to us." Holt drew a breath. "Would you mind walking us through the events that lead to the suspect's death?"

Gray could smell the bullshit in the air, but he sucked it up and gave a detailed accounting of what happened that night.

"And everything you've said here and in your report is correct to the best of your knowledge?"

"That's right."

DSU Hall cleared his throat. "Special Agent Gray, was there at any time during your physical altercation where you believe you could have prevented the death of the suspect?"

Gray had had a feeling that question was coming. It always did. *They're armchair quarterbacks making assumptions with hindsight on their side. The last time any of these uniforms were on the front lines was ages ago. They forget so fast.*

"I had seconds to make a decision to save my life and that of Ms. Pratt, who was already unconscious. I believe at that moment, I made the right decision."

DSU Hall looked around the table. "Does anybody have any further questions for Special Agent Gray?"

The room was silent, and Gray figured he was in the clear until he heard a familiar voice. It was his supervisor, Cooper. He was on the speakerphone listening in on the meeting. Yet no one thought to mention that.

"Special Agent Gray," Cooper said, "in your previous investigation, your suspect also ended up dead. I just think there's a little concern that a pattern might be forming. But with that said, I do think you made the right call. That's all I have to say."

This wasn't the first time Gray was on the receiving end of one of Cooper's backhanded compliments. The guy defined passive-aggressiveness.

"Right, then," DCI Holt said. "A big congratulations to everyone involved. Special Agent Gray, we do appreciate your assistance. You're welcome back at the Metropolitan Police anytime. And I don't believe I'm overstepping when I say our liaisons at Interpol are equally satisfied."

The uniforms cleared out of the conference room quickly without so much as a second look, leaving Gray, Gaston, and Pratt a little dumbfounded.

Pratt reached over to the speakerphone and switched it off. "Why were we asked to be in this meeting? All they did was question Sterling."

"I haven't the faintest idea," Gaston said. "But it seems like we're all in the clear."

"Hey, I won't push the issue," Gray said. "Gaston, it seems your superiors are happy. I believe the same is true of yours as well." Gray looked at Pratt. "I say, why rock the boat? Now, about that dinner tonight, is there anything I can bring?"

Later that evening, Gray and Gaston showed up at Pratt's home with a bottle of wine and a bouquet of flowers.

"Hello, Sterling. Hello, Chi," Evie said, and escorted the two men to a sitting room.

"Evie, how are you holding up?" Gray asked.

"I'm doing well. Knowing Eddie won't be able to do what he did to me and those other women ever again is huge relief. I can't thank you two enough for all you've done."

"No thanks needed. We're just doing our job."

"Well, if that's the case, how about we open that bottle of wine and whet our appetites? Lillie made a roast."

"I could smell it from outside," Gaston said as he rubbed his hands together.

"Hey, guys." Pratt entered the room wearing an apron.

"They brought flowers and wine." Evie held up the items.

"That's so sweet. Dinner will be ready in about fifteen minutes. You can settle in in the dining room."

"I can't wait. It smells delicious," Gray said.

Not once during dinner did the subject of Eddie or the investigation come up again. The four were too busy telling stories about their pasts. Gray talked about his tours of duty. Evie and Pratt told their story of how they met. And Gaston had more funny cheese stories than one could imagine.

"Sterling, when are you off to the States?" Evie asked.

"My flight's leaving at noon tomorrow."

"Oh, so soon."

"Too bad you couldn't stick around a little longer," Gaston said. "I got a pub I'd meant to take you to."

"You and your pubs."

Gray's phone rang. It was Cooper calling.

"Excuse me. I need to take this."

Gray stood and walked into the sitting room for a bit of privacy.

"Gray speaking."

"It's Cooper. I just wanted to tell you that everyone in London is thrilled with your performance there. You seem to have made quite the impression."

"They're a great team to work with, and I would definitely be open to working with them again."

"I'm happy to hear you say that. There's a tremendous opportunity for you there. You've shown what the BAU is capable of in a domestic capacity and on the international stage. How do you feel about staying on?"

"What do you mean by staying on? Like working on future investigations here in London?"

"Exactly, but permanently. You'll assist Interpol on investigations around the world. Could be very exciting stuff, and great for your career."

"Uh, well . . . I'm not sure. It's a lot to take in at the moment. Just to clarify, you're talking about relocating to London, right? Not coming and going for specific assignments?"

"That's correct. You would be working alongside Interpol on their investigations full time."

"Is Pratt aware of this?"

"I don't believe she's been made aware of it yet, but you would most likely be working with her. Is that a problem?"

"Uh, no. Just inquiring because it's very sudden."

"Indeed."

"When would you need an answer by? I'd like to give this some thought."

"Not a problem; I fully understand. It's a big decision. But luckily, with the time off you'll have coming up, you'll have plenty of time to think it over."

"Time off? What are you talking about?"

"Your use of deadly force. A suspect died at your hands."

"Wait a minute—I thought I was all but cleared of this in the meeting at the Met headquarters."

"You are, as far as our friends at the Met are concerned, but you still need to go through the formalities on our end. You'll need to ride a desk for six months, maybe longer. It depends."

"But you know I did nothing wrong."

"I know that. But the powers that be must also be made comfortable with it. Look, Gray, I know it's not right, but that's what will happen when you come back. You'll be at a desk, and you won't be assigned to any open investigations. It's a terrible waste of your time."

"It just makes no sense to be cleared here and not back at home."

"It doesn't. Interpol can assign you to as many investigations as they want, but I can't. It's this damn bureaucracy, but that's the way it is."

Right then, Gray realized what Cooper was really saying. If he wanted to avoid sitting at a desk for six months, he'd have to accept Cooper's proposal of staying in London and consulting for Interpol. It was total bullshit, but that was the position he had just been put in. Doing a great job got him more than an *attaboy* and a slap on the back. Cooper was going to deploy Gray at his disposal to make the BAU look good, which meant Cooper would look good. This was all about him and his continued climb to the top of the Bureau.

"Look, Gray, you did fine work on the last two investigations. I'm damn proud of you. Why don't you take a few days off and relax in London? Get acquainted. Take in the sights. The Bureau will cover the stay."

The transition had already started. Gray didn't have a decision to make. Cooper had already made it, and the paperwork was in motion. The phone call was just Cooper's way of breaking the news. Gray could stay in London and assist Interpol or he could come back stateside and ride a desk for as long as Cooper demanded. It was career suicide.

"Working on investigations around the world; that does sound tempting," Gray said.

"They say variety is the spice of life. You'll get plenty of that. It'll make you a better agent."

And it'll make you a much more promising candidate for director of the FBI. "I'm sure I'll learn a lot. I think I'll take you up on your offer to relax for a few days and get acquainted."

"Great. I'll hold off on that desk business for now. No need to rush the paperwork, right? Enjoy yourself, Gray. And good luck."

THE KING SNAKE
A STERLING GRAY FBI PROFILER NOVEL

When a sadistic human trafficker leads the kidnapping of an Interpol agent, only FBI profiler Sterling Gray can get inside his head...if Gray can stay alive long enough to do it.

The authorities have finally captured Somsak Ritthirong, the most dangerous human trafficker in Southeast Asia. Agent Gray takes the opportunity to interview him, hoping to gain insight into the man who committed so many human atrocities.

When he's invited to tag along for Ritthirong's extradition to Thailand, Gray doesn't expect to use any of his new knowledge—until Interpol Liaison Lillie Pratt is taken hostage.

Gray joins forces with a local detective to use his profiling skills to track down the people behind the missing agent, embarking on a wild cat-and-mouse chase across Thailand.

As dangerous forces close in from all directions, will Agent Gray uncover the truth in time to save Lillie Pratt from becoming another victim in Ritthirong's brutal business?

Get your copy today at
severnriverbooks.com/series/sterling-gray-fbi-profiler

ABOUT THE AUTHORS

Brian Shea has spent most of his adult life in service to his country and local community. He honorably served as an officer in the U.S. Navy. In his civilian life, he reached the rank of Detective and accrued over eleven years of law enforcement experience between Texas and Connecticut. Somewhere in the mix he spent five years as a fifth-grade school teacher. Brian's myriad of life experience is woven into the tapestry of each character's design. He resides in New England and is blessed with an amazing wife and three beautiful daughters.

Ty Hutchinson is a USA Today best seller. Since 2013, Ty has been traveling nonstop worldwide, all while banging away on his laptop and cranking out international crime and action thrillers. Immersing himself in different cultures, especially the food, is a passion that often finds its way into his stories.

Sign up for the reader list at
severnriverbooks.com/series/sterling-gray-fbi-profiler